BLOOD OF MY ENEMY

THE HUNTER GAMES

BOOK ONE

ARIEL DAWN

NAUGHTY NIGHTS PRESS LLC • CANADA

Sale of this book without a front cover may be unauthorized. If this book is coverless, it may have been reported to the publisher as "unsold or destroyed" and neither the author nor the publisher may have received payment for it.

No part of this book may be adapted, stored, copied, reproduced or transmitted in any form or by any means, electronic or mechanical, including photocopying, recording, or by any information storage and retrieval system, without permission in writing from the publisher.

Thank you for respecting the hard work of this author.

Blood Of My Enemy

The Hunter Games

Book One

Copyright ©2022 Ariel Dawn

ISBN: 978-1-77357-446-2

978-1-77357-447-9

Naughty Nights Press LLC

Cover Design by Willsin Rowe

Names, characters and incidents depicted in this book are products of the author's imagination or are used fictitiously. Any resemblance to actual events, locales, organizations, or persons, living or dead, is entirely coincidental and beyond the intent of the author.

BLOOD OF MY ENEMY

When the moon rises, the creatures of the night come out to play...

The hunt is all Malcolm Crowley—scratch that, Malcolm Reynolds—knows. Ever since Mal was thrust into a world of blood, enemies, and death, he's thought of nothing except revenge against the vampires who killed his parents and marked his sister. When a routine vamp hunt leads Mal and his fellow band of hunters—affectionately known as The Goon Squad—to a small town in the Blue Ridge Mountains, he discovers vampires aren't the only monsters he has to worry about.

BLOOD OF MY ENEMY

Clementine Srirocco longs for freedom. Freedom to run, to choose her own mate, instead of being beholden to the heat that determines her destiny as an Omega. When Cleo's heat is stirred by a chance meeting with a mortal—a dangerous hunter—both of their lives will be forever changed.

Can Mal and Cleo fight the bonds of fate?

Blood Of My Enemy is book one in The Hunter Games series, filled with hungry hunters, vicious vampires, wicked werewolves, and other supernatural creatures.

The enemy of my enemy is my friend.
—Ancient Sanskrit Proverb

Hell is empty and all the devils are here.
—William Shakespeare

1

MAL SAT AT the bar of the Lonestar Tavern, nursing his fourth or fifth whiskey of the evening. Alone.

Well, it wasn't as if he was *alone* alone. After all, Dallas was in the corner shooting pool with Vinny, and Tito and Hunter were still around somewhere, though he'd lost track of them. The red leather tops of the seat were practically molded to his ass, and despite it being

BLOOD OF MY ENEMY

eleven o'clock on a Friday night, there was barely anyone in the bar, let alone anyone who looked decent enough to talk to or hit on.

Not that Malcolm did a lot of *hitting* on anyone. That was more Dallas's department.

"I'd ask if you want to talk about it, but..." The bartender, who looked to be about in her mid-forties, spoke to him, and Mal scowled.

"I'm not the talking type, thanks," he answered.

"Suit yourself, wise guy, I was just—"

Mal slapped a few bills on the table, figuring now was as good a time as ever to leave. He hated making small talk, even when he was sober. But after a few drinks, he was always worried he'd let something slip.

ARIEL DAWN

"Thanks," he bit as he pushed away from the bar, feeling the effects of his drink. He blinked momentarily, his vision blurring only slightly.

They'd been in Stonyfield, Connecticut for three days already and still hadn't been able to locate the nest of vampires they sought after.

Knowing that until they found the nest, the risk and the deaths would not stop, only aggravated him.

He stumbled into a brick wall dressed in jeans and a blue flannel.

"Get the fuck out of my way, Dallas," Mal grumbled.

"And just where the hell do you think you're going?" Dallas set his hand on Mal's shoulder, raising an eyebrow at him.

"Home." Mal tried to shrug out of his

grasp, but Dallas's grip was solid.

"Let me drive you." His voice was serious.

"No." Mal grabbed his arm and pulled it off of him. "I'll be fine, I need the fresh air," Mal spoke.

"Malcolm..."

"Just let me go, Dallas. You're not my fucking mother." Mal exited the bar, Dallas hot on his tail.

"No, I'm not, but that doesn't mean I'm going to let you do something stupid. You're my friend, Mal, and I'd be a shitty partner if I let you run off into the woods buzzed and pissed with a plethora of weapons on you," Dallas said with a sigh.

Mal could hear the jingle of car keys, and as the cold air hit his face, he felt rather dizzy.

ARIEL DAWN

Soon it would be snowing and he'd have to relinquish walking around in just a flannel and band tees and pull out his parka. But tonight, Stonyfield felt less like the arctic and more like home.

Like Chester, Virginia.

Though truthfully, that wasn't really *home.*

Home was in Salem, Massachusetts and he hadn't seen it since he was twenty-six.

"Just let me go, I'll be fine!" Mal spun around, shoving Dallas, and as soon as he did it, he knew it was the wrong thing to do.

"Okay, that's it, get in the car, asshole." Dallas gripped Mal by the shoulder and all but dragged him to the sleek, candy apple red Chevelle, throwing him in the passenger seat.

BLOOD OF MY ENEMY

Even sober, Mal knew he couldn't really fight the mountain of a man that was Jake Dallas. After all, Dallas had been the wide receiver for his college team, and the man had him both in strength and body mass now, what with all his extra time in the gym everywhere they went. It was almost as if he was hiding something or trying to work something out. Dallas was like that. He'd rarely talk about the things that haunted him, and Mal knew better than to push or pry. Hitting the boxing bag until his knuckles were bleeding seemed to be the best approach for his friend.

Mal groaned as Dallas slammed the door, getting in the driver's seat.

"Quit fucking pouting," Dallas said as he started up the Chevelle, the roar of the engine coming to life. Mal could feel

ARIEL DAWN

the vibrations in the soles of his boots, and he huffed in annoyance.

"I'm not *pouting*," he said defensively.

Dallas reached for the radio dials, searching through the static until he found a station that was clear enough to make out the songs.

The familiar guitar riffs of "(Don't Fear) The Reaper" filled the air, and Malcolm could feel his muscles relax almost instantly.

"Mom loved this song," he drawled as he leaned back against the seat, closing his eyes.

In his vision, it was almost as if he could see her, touch her. Like she was still somehow here.

The smell of dead leaves and moist earth was most potent, mixing with the sweet lure of fresh-baked apple turnovers

BLOOD OF MY ENEMY

wafting through the screen door from the kitchen. The air had already chilled, and it was a perpetual marathon of rain and cloudy skies, which only added to the overall appeal and aesthetic of Salem.

His mother, Lenora Crowley, sat on the porch with the radio, the porch swing creaking with every rocking motion she caused.

Malcolm took a hit of his cigarette, blowing smoke in the air, just as his mother did the same. The familiar lyrics echoed all around them.

"When are you going to learn this one?" she asked as Malcolm watched the gray tendrils of smoke curl in the air.

"You say that about every song that comes on the radio," he teased as he tapped the butt into the ashtray precariously balanced on the metal ledge

ARIEL DAWN

of the porch sofa.

"But this one is my favorite," she said as she rocked the swing, the squeaky creaks interrupting the perfectly sung lyrics.

"This was the song that was playing the—"

"Night you met Dad, I know. You've told me," he said, his tone slightly annoyed.

Lenora twisted her lips as she flicked her cigarette in the ashtray set on the concrete wall of the front porch.

"I don't need a rehash of how you weren't supposed to go to the concert, but you did," he said as he looked out over the porch at the picturesque sunset, enjoying the way the sun melted into the clouds, gold and reds seeping into the horizon until they disappeared

BLOOD OF MY ENEMY

completely.

"One day you'll understand," she mumbled. Mal continued to watch the sun, noticing as a few stray silhouettes of bikes rode off into the distance.

The memory was still so vivid to him, despite the fact it'd happened so many years ago. In fact, he replayed it in his mind over and over again quite frequently, being as it was the last time he'd seen her alive. The last time he'd been ignorant to the world that was now his reality.

The haunting melody pained him just as much as it soothed him. Malcolm shifted in his seat, feeling restless, all the anger and all the guilt rushing back.

I should have been there.

If I would have been there, they'd still be alive…

ARIEL DAWN

Mal's thoughts were pulled from his melancholy musing when the purr of his engine stopped and the tinkling of keys alerted him that they'd reached their destination. A part of him wished to stay put in his car, for it was the only place he felt truly safe. He'd called the Chevelle home for the last fifteen years, since...

Mal ran a hand over his face, trying to banish the images, the memories from his brain. But it was no use. He wasn't nearly drunk enough to do so, and for that, he cursed himself.

His door swung open, and he looked up at the towering force that stood before him.

"We going to do this the easy way or the hard way tonight?" Dallas said as he leaned against the doorframe, his

BLOOD OF MY ENEMY

expression tired and annoyed.

"I told you, I can take care of my-myself..." Malcolm huffed as he swung at Dallas, wishing he would disappear.

Wishing all of it would disappear, fade into the background, and he could be *free.*

Free from the guilt, free from the blood. Free from the revenge that fueled him, free from the responsibility of making sure the only family he had left was safe.

Free to live life like a normal, happy thirty-one-year-old man with a nice garage, a white picket fence, and a wife and kids. But such things were not in the cards for Malcolm Crowley, no. And he suspected they never would be.

Fucking bloodsuckers took everything from me...

ARIEL DAWN

Dallas grasped his wrist, holding it tightly, and Malcolm grunted angrily.

"The hard way it is then," Dallas said through heavy breath as Malcolm stumbled out of the car, taking another swing. Dallas let go of his arm, the two sparring in the chilly night amidst the glow of the parking lot of the Motel 6. It didn't take much effort until Dallas had Malcolm pressed against him, twisting his arm behind his back. Mal let out a gruff sound but Dallas held him still.

"Let go of me!" Malcolm growled out.

"Stop acting like a bitch," Dallas said with no inflection.

Mal twisted in his grasp, his breath coming in heavier now, his mind spinning.

Blood.

There was so much blood...

BLOOD OF MY ENEMY

Blood in his memories, blood on his hands. They'd lost their targets, they were too late. And because of it, people were going to die.

And they were no closer to finding the vamp who murdered his parents, or any leads on how to cure Ava of her claim mark.

He was angry.

So very angry.

The solid force of Dallas against him was like being trapped against a brick wall with nowhere to go. In his grip, he knew if he resisted too much, he'd only end up hurting himself. The cold air against his skin grounded him to the here and now, and his body heated as the memories replayed, as his slideshow of failure rose to the surface, causing his stomach to churn.

ARIEL DAWN

I think I'm going to be sick...

"Fuck you," he said, his words tinged with sadness, anger, and most of all... pain.

"You couldn't handle *a* dick, let alone *this dick* even if you wanted to," Dallas taunted him, actually letting out a laugh, and suddenly it was like a breath of fresh air.

Malcolm couldn't help but let out a strained laugh of his own at his words.

Dallas was the furthest thing from gay, but that didn't stop him from cracking jokes, especially when the situation called for it.

It was one of the things Malcolm truly appreciated about his partner and friend. His ability to cut through all the bullshit and reach him when it felt as if no one could help, as if he was better off

BLOOD OF MY ENEMY

alone.

They stood there in the dark of night, laughing under the glow of the Motel 6 sign. When Dallas finally let go, Malcolm leaned against the car and sighed.

"I don't know about you, but I'm fucking beat, man," he said as he ran his hand over his face.

Dallas only nodded as he locked the car door before leading Mal back to their shitty hotel room, where Malcolm finally let the darkness consume him.

2

MAL PINCHED THE space between his eyes as the bright sunlight beamed down on him, its heat like a damn spotlight. The birds chirping happily in the morning's glow irritated him as the sound was borderline shrilling.

Tito sunk his hands into his bomber jacket, the wind rustling his blond hair almost as if he were some supermodel instead of a vampire slayer. Hunter was

BLOOD OF MY ENEMY

taking his time returning with their breakfast, something Mal was acutely aware of as he had woken up with an insatiable hunger for something carb heavy and caffeinated.

When he'd awakened, he was alone, though it was not abnormal for him. He spent most of his mornings alone, knowing how much Dallas favored his runs, especially after they had lost a fight.

The guilt flooded him once more, about how they'd lost the vampires. How they'd evaded them again. As if the thought alone could rouse such things, his stomach twisted just as Vinny set the map out on the hood of his red Chevelle, nearly knocking him over.

"Excuse you," Mal grumbled as Vinny smoothed out the map, clicking his tongue as his fingers scoured the tiny lines and routes. Despite the fact he was the same age as Ava, Vinny was not one for all the draws of technology. In fact, he insisted he was cursed when it came to such things, and Mal had seen enough to wonder if it were true at times. Power outages in the middle of the day, smartphones that would endlessly spin and never load their websites, or on the odd occasion, apps and programs that just stopped working.

Vinny didn't even flinch at his grumble. Instead, he just kept on in Vinny Mode like he always did.

The man had an almost uncanny ability when it came to studying and mapping out locations. They all had talents, and Vinny's was details.

Tito was more skilled with a set of

knives than a butcher and a damn good bassist, while Hunter was as good with research and lore as Vinny was with maps. Dallas wasn't just the oldest of their band of misfits, he was the strongest, though clearly not always the smartest. Dallas's temper had aided them on many occasions, but it had also landed them in hot water more than once.

Which was where Malcolm always came in: Captain Charisma. He'd always been quite the charmer, the talker. Able to maneuver his way in and out of things with a smile and some fancy talking, and when talking didn't do the trick, his stake would.

"Hunter and I got a call from our friend, Jones, last night..."

"And he was up all freaking night

ARIEL DAWN

clamoring away like some of us weren't trying to sleep," Tito drawled as Vinny shot him an annoyed glare.

Mal couldn't help but crack a smile, a laugh begging to be let loose. Vinny was always so tightly wound when it came to things that it was almost too easy to rile him up—a feat Tito was more than good at—and yet, it never seemed to get old. But if anyone tried to mess with their own personal MapQuest, Mal would personally roll some heads. Their "Goon Squad"—as his sister called them—was the closest thing he had to family. Well, outside of his sister and his aunt, but that was different.

"Looks like they got some evidence up their way of some deaths they think might be caused by vamps. Could be our band of bats making their way through,"

BLOOD OF MY ENEMY

Vinny said as he pointed to a small dot on the map. "They're just outside of Mahoning, which, by my calculations, is about an eight hour drive from here," Vinny explained matter-of-factly, in the most positive tone one could muster at this early hour.

Mal tried to focus his vision, but it was still slightly blurry due to his migraine and the sun.

Where the fuck is Hunter with my damn coffee?

"Isn't Mahoning pretty much all forest?" Dallas's voice boomed from behind, making them all turn in unison.

Dallas wiped his brow with his muscle tank, which he'd taken off at some point in his run, more than likely. The sun made his sweat glisten, making him look almost like some kind of motorcycle god, his double-star tattoos looking darker against his tanned skin.

Before Mal could speak, Hunter appeared behind him, carrying a plastic bag full of breakfast and a carrier of coffees in hand.

"It's about fucking time, Hunter. Thought I was going to have to go kill breakfast my damn self," Mal grumbled as he swiped a coffee from the carrier like an eagle snatches a rabbit.

Hunter grunted in annoyance. "I've been gone literally fifteen minutes, Mal, cool your jets."

"He can't cool anything, he's nursing another hangover," Tito said completely deadpan.

"How's that different from any other morning?" Vinny asked seriously.

All of them turned to look at Vinny

BLOOD OF MY ENEMY

with the same don't-go-there look, the black-haired, tracking savant completely dumbfounded as usual. The man just didn't know when not to say something. A trait that combined with Dallas's temper was quite a wild card.

"And to answer your question, Dallas, yes. Mahoning borders the Highlands, which is basically all mountains."

"I hate the fucking mountains," Mal said as he sipped his coffee. The bitter taste on his tongue was like a shock to his system, making him feel a fraction better from the strong taste alone.

The mountains were never his favorite place to be when he was young, mostly because he hated the wide open, endless maze of forest and all the sounds that came with it, but he'd tolerated it during the family camping

ARIEL DAWN

trips he'd been forced to take before his sister was born.

Now, the mountains reminded him of them—his parents. Everything reminded him of them.

"What would a bunch of vampires want up there? Mahoning's tiny, can't imagine there's much blood there they could pick that wouldn't draw attention," Hunter said as he set the box of donuts on top of Vinny's map, popping it open. The smell of fresh-glazed sugar was practically mouthwatering and Dallas nearly crashed into him as they both dove for the sole chocolate one.

"Back off, it's mine," Malcolm growled at Dallas.

"Fuck it is," Dallas said as he swiped it from the box in one clean, fell swoop, Malcolm cursing all the while.

BLOOD OF MY ENEMY

Vinny grabbed a pink-frosted donut, unfazed by the immature posturing aside him.

"Who knows what the hell they are headed there for, but everything I've studied up until this point, and every which way I look at it, it all comes back to this. There's nothing else remotely close that isn't all woods at this point. They could go around it, but why would they? It's the closest town for miles. They might be bloodsucking ticks, but they still need to eat and pass as humans, right? If it's our band of bloodsuckers, then we might finally be able to catch them. The five of us, plus Jones…"

"You think we have a shot?" Mal asked as the coffee started to settle his nerves and the tension in his head abated.

ARIEL DAWN

"If it's our vamps, they are a small group. Probably not more than four or five, based on the evidence we have with the bodies they've left. We can take them, and they won't have anywhere to go. They'll be forced to hide out in the town during the day."

"And what if it's not vampires?" Hunter asked, raising an eyebrow.

Tito rolled his eyes. "What else could it be, *el tonto*?" he asked with disdain.

"Well, for starters... we've seen an Incubus 'fake' a vampire kill. Who's to say some other supernatural freakshow wouldn't do the same thing? Draw attention to something else so they could keep doing what they are," Hunter said with a shrug as he took a drink of his coffee.

"Such as?" Dallas crossed his arms,

and Mal took another pull of his coffee.

The sun had disappeared behind the clouds for a moment, casting a gray haze over the boys and the car just as a gentle breeze blew through, bringing with it the beginning of autumn chill.

"There are numbers of fanged creatures. Djinn, faeries, mermaids, manticore—"

"Narrow it down to the *likely* suspects, Hunt," Mal breathed out in annoyance, catching the young man mid-ramble.

"I mean, it could be a demon or a werewolf. Those are the two most likely fanged culprits."

"I've been hunting longer than you've been out of the fucking womb, trust me when I say werewolves aren't real. If they were, we'd have pinched one, or at the very least, heard about one from another hunter by now," Dallas said as he finished licking the chocolate off his fingers.

Asshole.

"Just because you cannot see it, doesn't mean it does not exist, *el cabron*," Tito said as he started twirling his knives, obviously bored with the conversation.

"It's vampires," Mal spoke up, knowing he needed to rein them all in and get everyone back on the same page. With the caffeine in his system and his headache starting to ease as he picked up a powdered donut, he knew it was best to keep moving. It was the only logical conclusion. If Mahoning was the only place around for miles until the other side of the Blue Ridge mountains,

BLOOD OF MY ENEMY

the vamps would have to stop there regardless. And if they were there feasting, they'd likely be hibernating until dark, which would give them all enough time to get in, slay the ticks, and maybe have a beer afterward.

"Everyone get your shit and get ready to rock. We're going to the mountains."

3

DALLAS WAS FOCUSED on his phone as Mal continued to drive a steady seventy on the long, abandoned road toward the trees in the distance. He'd noticed Dallas had been particularly attentive to it today, almost as if he was waiting for something, some news or alert.

"What's your deal today? You've been staring at that thing like you're some goddamned teenager," he said.

Dallas quickly closed the screen, setting it on the dashboard and nodding in return.

"What else am I supposed to look at on this trip? Your face?"

"Very funny," Mal said as he rolled his eyes, focusing back on the road. "I thought maybe you had a stage-five clinger or something you were waiting to text once you were out of the fucking state," he said with a laugh.

The drive always helped focus his mind, ever since he was a teenager. There was something about the steady rhythm of the engine as it purred beneath him, the way his surroundings blurred and faded into each other, colors meshing and meddling like spilled, runny paint into one another until they'd

ARIEL DAWN

become indistinguishable from what they were before.

Somewhere in the middle of all of it, Malcolm felt at peace.

They'd been driving for nearly six hours, and at the rate they were going, they'd get to Mahoning earlier than they anticipated. For once, it seemed as if Lady Luck was on their side.

"No, not this time," Dallas said. Though his face didn't betray any inkling something was off, Malcolm thought he sounded different. Almost as if he was unsure of what to say, which was weird.

Dallas wasn't afraid of anything, least of all talking about the countless women he wound up in bed with.

The man was the epitome of a chick magnet, and Mal acknowledged on more than one occasion that had it not been for the band or his dreamboat-esque wingman, Mal likely would have had a more serious relationship with his right hand.

Dallas shifted in his seat, looking out the window, and Mal decided to let it go. Whatever had Dallas in a mood, he didn't want to press. He'd talk about it when he wanted to, *if* he wanted to talk at all.

So when the former wide receiver spoke up, breaking the silence, Mal was surprised.

"Have you talked to your sister lately? You know, since you left after Terror Con."

Dallas's words shocked him, and he gripped his steering wheel a little tighter.

"Of course I've talked to her," he answered plainly.

ARIEL DAWN

"I mean about hunting... again." Dallas's words were careful, almost as if he was walking a tight rope, and that unnerved Mal. He was starting to feel better from his hangover from hell, but this made him feel anything but.

Truth be told, it wasn't that Malcolm didn't want to talk to her—it was more that he didn't want to argue with her.

After she'd been bitten by the Incubus—the possessed celebrity ghost hunter Sam Kingsley—she'd come close to death. In a burning building, the Incubus's venom had taken hold—but the ritual hadn't been completed. It was just a matter of luck that he'd had the anti-venom, that they'd been able to deliver it in enough time, and that Cassius's friend had provided them somewhere safe to do so. Though, he

BLOOD OF MY ENEMY

wouldn't thank the bloodsucking Aurelia even on his deathbed. Though Cassius hadn't moved to finish the job he started, Mal knew he was smart. Smarter than most vampires he'd met, anyway. He could not trust the leech, not when it came to his sister.

He wasn't stupid, he knew the vampire held affection for her—after all, he'd claimed her. The bond that existed between them only exacerbated the attraction. Thankfully, it was only one-sided and Ava was putting up a hell of a fight, but they'd run out of time, eventually.

It was easier to keep Ava out of sight and out of mind while he searched for a way to do just that, save her. But Dallas was right. Eventually, she'd start to grow antsy, and she'd need to kill again, just as he did. As much as he didn't like to admit it, he and his sister were cut from the same cloth.

Genetics and all that.

Mal pursed his lips as the thoughts filled his brain. He'd rationalized with himself that she knew the risks, they all did every time they took their weapon in their hands and went chasing after the monsters in the darkness.

So why did the thought of her taking up her stake again leave him feeling panicked and afraid?

"There are more important things she needs to worry about, right now. Like finishing college," Mal huffed out.

"You can't sideline her forever, Mal. You can try, but trust me when I say she'll just end up doing something to piss you off in the long run."

BLOOD OF MY ENEMY

Mal focused on the trees. The shades of red and orange faded into the dying green. He needed to find some peace since the conversation was making him feel pissed off.

"I'm not sidelining her, I just—" Mal let out a deep breath, his pulse increasing with every thought, every word. "She can be pissed at me all she wants. She's my sister and it's my job to keep her safe. My job—"

Dallas ran a hand through his dark hair. "I get it, man. Believe me. But she's not some doe-eyed twat who doesn't know shit. She's trained. *We* trained her. And you know she's not half bad, and you know she has her own demons to chase, to—"

"Why are we talking about this? What do you care all of a sudden about what

ARIEL DAWN

my sister does or doesn't do?"

Dallas paused for a moment, the air thick with tension between them.

Tension that made Mal nervous.

He stepped on the gas, needing to control something before he lost his own temper.

"She's in more danger sitting like a duck in Chester with that fucking vampire swirling her than she would be if she were to be on the road, hunting. With us."

Mal took his exit rather quickly, jostling the large hunter in his seat and nearly giving him whiplash.

"The fuck, man, take it easy!" Dallas grumbled as he righted himself just as Malcolm pulled off to the side of the road. The sun shone through the windshield, lighting Dallas up in its

BLOOD OF MY ENEMY

golden beams, and Mal couldn't deny the sinking feeling in his gut.

"She's in danger *because* of me..." Mal started to speak as Dallas breathed out a heavy sigh.

"You can't keep blaming yourself, man. You can't keep doing this." Dallas's voice was serious, and Mal opened his mouth to speak, but Dallas continued. "Ava isn't your parents. What happened to them..." His voice caught in his throat, a sound that made Malcolm all the more angry, all the more frustrated. "She's sharp, focused, and scrappy as hell. Like you. I've met a lot of hunters in my time, so I can tell you, without a doubt, that she is one of the good ones, Mal. She's got so much fucking potential. Just like you did when I met you. She's capable of so much more than you give her credit for. Fight *with* her. Not against her."

Just at that moment, as the words kissed the air, Mal felt a vibration in his pocket. He didn't have to pull his phone out to look at the owner of the notification. After all, there were very few people he associated with, let alone gave his number to. One was in the car with him, three were behind him, and the last had an uncanny ability to always pop up when he didn't want to deal with her at all. He slid the phone out of his pocket slowly and looked to see "Simba" calling.

Mal looked at Dallas, his eyes dark as he stowed away his counterargument for the moment and accepted the call.

"Ava," he greeted her calmly, his voice never betraying the worry, the anger, or the helplessness he truly felt.

BLOOD OF MY ENEMY

Dallas opened the door, leaning his large frame out. "I'm going to take a piss," he said, not looking at Mal, not giving him any chance to respond. Ava's voice took over his concentration, her words hitting him like a ton of bricks.

"What do you mean you are on a case? By yourself?"

4

THE VOICES OUTSIDE Cleo's window were loud. Alaric and Sawyer were always loud, though. That was just who they were. Both of them were tall, over six foot, and had the same appearance to them that most of the men did when it came to their species. The same, sun-kissed complexion, the same build, the same feral look in their eyes. Hell, they even dressed alike, not that there was much reason to wear colorful prints or designer goods when they were in the middle of the woods, removed from nearly everything. Not when they were all trying to fit in, to go unnoticed.

Cleo pulled her legs up to her chest, setting her chin on her knees, her blue-green eyes dancing around her room. It was a beautiful room. The Thornes had truly done a lovely job making the place cozy. The egg-shaped wicker chair with soft, furry blankets, the large, pillowy, king-size bed that was bigger than anything she'd ever seen and more comfortable than her bed back home across the ridge.

But it wasn't home, and it never would be.

She sighed deeply, remembering her small, yet warm home. The scent of her

ARIEL DAWN

mother's soups on the stove, the sound of her father's records. The man was always playing music, and their home was always so alive with joy because of it.

A knock on her door alerted her and she jumped, her thoughts dissipating. She looked to see it was the youngest of the Thorne brothers, Rocky. She relaxed instantly as her gaze fell on him. His features were similar to his older siblings', but where their eyes were shimmering blue like the sky, Rocky's were as green as the treetops in the forest.

"You didn't come down to dinner," he said as he crossed his arms, but his tone was soft, even.

"I wasn't hungry," Cleo said plainly, taking long strands of her dark, golden-streaked hair into her fingers, twisting them together in a braid, absentmindedly. She let her eyes fall away, breaking his gaze.

"That's too bad because my parents are out for the night," he said as he ran his hand through his hair. The motion actually made him look somewhat appealing, but it wasn't enough to stir the heat.

Nothing was strong enough to stir the heat, and Cleo worried every day that it wouldn't come.

How long will the Thornes wait?

What if it never comes?

"They are very brave to hunt when our enemies are doing the same," she said as she unfurled her legs, swinging them around to the side of the bed.

"I thought maybe we could grab a bite

to eat somewhere else."

Cleo couldn't help but smile at the mischievous smirk on Rocky's face. "Won't you get in trouble if you take me out of this house?" she asked sweetly, noting the blush in his cheeks.

"Not if we don't get caught," he answered smoothly.

Suddenly, the tension started to melt away, Cleo's curiosity piqued. "Is this a date, then?" she asked as she raised an eyebrow.

Rocky stood up straighter. "No. It's not... I mean... only if you want it to be. I mean... It can just be two friends hanging out. Getting to know each other," he said quickly.

Cleo nodded, finishing her braid. "What about your brothers?" she nodded to the window.

BLOOD OF MY ENEMY

Rocky's gaze darted to the spot and, as if on cue, the hooting and hollering of Alaric and Sawyer escalated as sounds of laughter erupted around them.

"I think they're pretty occupied with the rest of the pack, right now. You know, dumb alpha and beta shit," Rocky bit out.

In the weeks that she'd been a *guest* of the Thornes, she'd picked up on the underlying animosity Rocky held for his brothers.

Especially Alaric, the soon-to-be-alpha.

Her soon-to-be-mate.

That was, he would be her mate if she'd go into heat already. The Oracle had seen it plain as day. It had been far too long since the Thornes had an omega, and the Oracle had been very

ARIEL DAWN

clear that Cleo's arrival in Mahoning, her stay with the Thornes, would bring the heat. But it had been nearly three weeks and she'd barely left the house because not long after her arrival, *they* came.

The vampires.

What if we run into one of them, or more than one...

Cleo's conscience told her to be reasonable, to be safe. But Clementine Srirocco was not one to usually play by the rules. The only reason she hadn't tried to escape or sneak out before was because the elder Thornes kept a close eye on her.

"You know what, Rocky, I think I am a bit hungry, actually," she said with a smile.

"Great. I know just the place," he said as he turned around, looking at her over

BLOOD OF MY ENEMY

his shoulder.

Cleo jumped off the bed, strolling over to the twenty-two-year-old with burgeoning curiosity.

As they walked through to the garage, a shiver of worry coursed down her spine. She slid into the passenger seat of Rocky's Fiesta, scrunching herself down just in case they'd pass the older Thorne brothers on the way out.

"It's safe now," Rocky said with a smirk, once they'd pulled out from the long, dirt road that seemed to go on for miles until it reached their house in the forest.

Cleo sat up straighter, her momentary nerves but a memory when she saw the lights of the town come into view. Against the setting sun, the forest and the town looked like something out

ARIEL DAWN

of a movie.

Rocky pulled into the parking lot of Howler's just as another car came speeding in. "Holy hell, do you see that asshole?" Rocky said as they parked.

Cleo looked out the window, noting the men in the candy apple colored car had already vacated it and were well on their way into the bar.

"Yeah, maybe they're in a hurry," she said with a shrug as she moved to open her door.

"I'll get that, just sit tight," Rocky said as he scrambled in his seat, unbuckling his seat belt and practically bolting out of the car to open her door.

She sighed, once again wishing the heat would just show up already. The sooner it came, the sooner she could move on with her life. Even if moving on

BLOOD OF MY ENEMY

meant she'd become Alaric's mate.

Maybe I'll get lucky and it'll be Rocky...

She looked up at him as he held the car door open and offered her his hand.

He actually treats me like a person and not just an omega.

It wasn't uncommon for an omega to have a connection with the one who stirred their heat, but if they were mated to an alpha, such connections were frowned upon. At least Rocky would be in the same house, which wouldn't be so bad.

"Are you ready for some food and some fun?" he said with a bright smile, his voice hitching an octave, as if he was *trying* to sound cheesy.

Cleo set her hand in his palm and exited the car, taking in the sight of the

ARIEL DAWN

strewn lantern lights and the rustic picnic tables adorned with the little green ashtrays that reminded her of dark, green leaves of English ivy.

The sounds coming from the bar were full of laughter, joy, and thanks to her increased hearing, she could even make out the notes of *Bad Moon Rising* by CCR playing amidst it all. She'd always loved that song growing up because her father used to play it all the time on his record player, and perhaps, that is why she smiled, and why she felt like the tides might be changing.

The night was full of endless possibilities.

"Absolutely," she said.

5

THE WATER PRESSURE in the Moonflower Motel was piss-poor and too cold for Malcolm's liking.

Why was it that everyone seemed to be on board with Ava joining the hunt?

Was he really that out of touch with things?

No, he wasn't. He'd worked so hard to keep that life from touching her, from sinking its fangs in, but she'd been

BLOOD OF MY ENEMY

bitten regardless.

By an Aurelia.

Of all the vampires, all the creatures to be bound to, it had to be to the one breed of bloodsucker that could actually turn her—a fate worse than death.

Though he couldn't deny Dallas had a point. Ava *did* have a knack for slaying, just as he did. She'd helped him out twice, mostly on local jobs when he was home or close to it, when Dallas was off the case or when he needed to disappear for a few days to get his head back on straight.

Mal braced his hands against the chipped shower tiles, letting the cold water run down his face and his arms as he let out a deep sigh.

Maybe the others were right. Maybe it would be better if she was closer, in his line of sight, away from Cassius.

But the vampire had followed her all the way to Oklahoma before...

And then there was the matter of her mark. The claiming bite Cassius had placed on her drew other vampires out. That had been proven. Though it was stupid to challenge the claim, being as Cassius was a stronger, more rare breed of vampire than the general bloodsucker population, the bat brains still did it. They couldn't help themselves, and Malcolm couldn't understand it, either.

Vampires didn't wait to turn a human if they had the capability, so why hadn't Cassius made good on his mark yet?

The notion didn't sit right with him. No, instead, it scared him. Perhaps Cassius was waiting for them all to trust him, to become complacent in their

BLOOD OF MY ENEMY

bond, and then he would strike.

It certainly couldn't be anything else. After all, vampires did not have hearts or morals. They only desired one thing—blood. And they would stop at nothing to get it, to sink their fangs into human flesh, taking pleasure and life away in one fell swoop.

The idea of Ava *hunting* such things on her own scared him, given her vampire brand, just as much as the idea of her jumping back into the fray with backup, but he had to admit to himself that her vampire radar was rather handy. And if the others were right about the numbers, well, then drawing them out and slaying them would be a piece of cake.

He turned off the water, grabbing for a towel just as he heard the click of the

ARIEL DAWN

door.

Dallas must be back.

Checking his watch, Mal noticed they had nearly fifteen minutes before meeting with Jones at Howlers. He wrapped the towel around his waist before heading out into the room. His clothes and weaponry laid out on the bed before him, a startling contrast against the pale-blue comforter.

The Moonflower Motel looked like something from another era—all pale blues and beige with flourishes of mauve gave the place an eighties, early nineties feel, but the decor and the acrylic accents made it feel like something straight out of a 1950s textbook.

And don't even get me started on the damn flower paintings...

"Where have you been?" Mal said

gruffly as he pulled the towel from his waist, not giving two shits about showing his crown jewels off at the moment. He and Dallas had been traveling together for nearly six years. There wasn't much they hadn't seen of each other.

Dallas fingered through his duffel bag on the bed, looking for something.

"What are you? My fucking keeper now?" Dallas scoffed.

"Just making conversation, D."

"I'm sorry man, I just— I'm a little off right now."

Mal pulled his black shirt on, the motion ruffling his dark hair. "I know. I also know you're not one to talk about shit, but if you need to, you know you can."

Dallas fell back on the bed, looking

ARIEL DAWN

up at the popcorn ceiling. With his size, he practically took up the entire thing. "I actually called the manager of Howlers. Asked if maybe they had a spot open we could play or something."

Mal blinked, slightly surprised at his words. Usually, they all discussed playing gigs, and it had been a while since they'd performed.

"I thought we were just here on vamp business," Mal said as he slid into his dark-wash jeans.

"I mean, we could always use the cash, right?" he said quietly.

"What happened? You blow the last of your paycheck on some fine ass or something?" Mal said humorously, knowing it wasn't *completely* out of tune for Dallas to do something of that nature, but it wasn't likely.

BLOOD OF MY ENEMY

In fact, if he was being honest, he hadn't seen Dallas hit on, flirt, or leave with *anyone* in the last year. But he didn't intend on asking him all the details. Whatever was going on with Dallas and his sex life was none of his business.

"I just miss playing sets. We used to play a lot more, but ever since—" The silence that fell between them was palpable. "Ever since we found out about Ava's bite, it just kind of seems like it's vampires and demons twenty-four-seven, and I just want a break, man."

Mal sat on the bed next to his friend, his partner, as the words hung in the air. He was right.

Ever since Mal had discovered what happened to his sister, *what* really bit her, he'd made it a top priority to find a

ARIEL DAWN

way to rid her of her death mark.

They'd followed leads that turned into nothing, tried herbs, chants, charms... Nothing had helped thus far, and they were running out of options. So of course, it was all he thought about when he wasn't picking off ticks. Trying to find the vampires who murdered his slayer parents and a cure for his bitten sister took up nearly ninety-five percent of his brain. The rest was committed to self-loathing, depression, and feeling like a complete failure.

The last time they'd played a show at all was before Terror Con, and his amp was collecting dust in the backseat of his Chevelle. Maybe Dallas was right. Maybe they all needed a little bit of R&R after this hunt.

After they'd burned the monsters to

BLOOD OF MY ENEMY

ash.

"What did he say?" Mal said as he ran his hand through his hair, down over his face. His rough facial hair brushed against his own palm, and he made a mental note to shave after the job was done as well.

"Said we could play tomorrow at nine, just give him a heads-up tonight when we come in."

Malcolm nodded in agreement. "I'm sure the others won't say no," he said, his lips turning up in the corners into a slight smile.

"Fuck no, they won't," Dallas said with a smile of his own.

"I miss it, too, you know. Just jamming with you guys. Makes me feel like, for an hour, I'm a completely normal person."

ARIEL DAWN

Dallas sat up, nudging his friend in the arm. "You are a normal person. Most normal person I know."

Malcolm let out a dark laugh. "Then I'm afraid you know a lot of psychopaths, my friend, if you think *I'm* the normal one."

Dallas laughed. "I mean, have you met Tito? That man is certifiable."

"Shit, we need to head out or we're going to be late. Tell me you know how to get to Howlers?" Mal asked as he sprang up from his seat.

Dallas nodded. "I mean, this town's tiny as hell, it can't be that hard to find the place," he said as he followed suit, the both of them climbing into the Chevelle, driving off into the setting sun.

***

BLOOD OF MY ENEMY

The bar known as Howlers was the epitome of a small-town dive bar. The warm, white lanterns strewn along the faded, red awning cast an almost pinkish glow, meddling with the blue and red neon signs in the tiny windows. There was outdoor seating, picnic tables with equally faded umbrellas, little mason jars with tealight candles, and green plastic ashtrays adorned all the tables. For nearly six on a Thursday night, it seemed as if the place was fairly busy.

"Guess this is the place," Mal said as he pushed through the door into the smoky room.

There was no band playing this evening, but there was a fully set stage, complete with a drum set in the center of the room. The unmistakable guitar riff of

ARIEL DAWN

CCR's *Bad Moon Rising* filled the air, amidst the chatter from a handful of locals at the bar, and dispersed throughout the dimly lit room. Posters that were practically peeling off the walls lined nearly every corner, and the wooden floor creaked as he walked, but strangely it was the most at home he'd ever felt on the road since he started hunting. There was something about this place that felt familiar, cozy even, to him.

"There they are," Dallas said as he made a beeline for a circular table near the back of the room, next to an old-fashioned looking jukebox.

"Well, well, finally decided to join us, I see," Tito said as he picked up his glass, sipping his beer. His dark eyes held no emotion, nor did his voice. Though that

BLOOD OF MY ENEMY

was just Tito; the man never showed any hint of emotion over anything.

Except when he was laying a stake into the chest of a bloodsucker, that was.

"Well, you know, I had to wait on this asshole to get back from taking a long-ass piss. Almost had to set a candle out for him in remembrance or some shit," Mal said with a smirk as he pulled up an empty chair, his gaze falling on the rest of his band mates before the unknown man in question. Jones didn't look much older than the rest of them in build or appearance, but upon closer look, Mal noticed the wrinkles up by his eyes. The way his tan, leathery knuckles looked almost swollen from cuts and bruises. The man clearly spent time outdoors, if his complexion and the sheen of dirt on

ARIEL DAWN

his jacket were any indication, and he could even see the beginnings of a beard forming on his face.

"You must be Jones," he said as he extended his hand.

Jones took it, his grip firm, and shook. "And you must be Malcolm. Vin's told me a lot about you," he said with a genuine smile.

Mal couldn't help but return it. "All good things, I hope," he said as he winked at Vinny, who let out a laugh of his own.

"Some," Vinny said as he held his glass up before taking a drink of his own beer.

"Don't believe everything you hear, the stories often don't do him justice," Dallas said as he turned the chair around, straddling the front.

BLOOD OF MY ENEMY

Mal rolled his eyes. "And this is my stage five clinger, Jake Dallas," he said with a nod to Jones. The other man chuckled.

"Bitch, you would be so lucky to have me up your ass. Would tear the smile right off your fucking face," Dallas guffawed, and everyone was chuckling. Soon enough, though, the laughter died down and silence fell as the jukebox finished out its tune.

"So the reason we're here—" Vinny started to speak, but Jones held his hand up.

"I know why you're here. After all, I called you, remember?" he said as he leaned back against the wall, his fingers trailing up and down his glass, which had a sip of whiskey left in it.

"You think you got a vamp problem?"

ARIEL DAWN

Hunter spoke up finally.

Jones nodded in response.

"All signs point to vamps, but—"

"But what?" Mal leaned closer, outstretching his arm on the table. The jukebox queued up its next song, the deep, classic sounds of *Spirit in the Sky* echoing in the air.

Jones fixed his gaze on Malcolm as he continued, "I can't put my finger on it. Something feels off, but then again, we haven't had vamps up this way in about a decade, so maybe I'm just rusty. That's why I called Vinny, I—"

Mal was most intrigued by his words.

"I know that's kind of your specialty," Jones said after finishing the remains of his drink.

"I guess our reputation proceeds us then," Mal said smugly.

BLOOD OF MY ENEMY

"Just so happens, we were tracking a band of vamps and we think they moved up this way. There isn't anything for miles, as you know, so we think they'll likely lay low and stock up on blood first, which gives us two, maybe three days tops to draw them out and trap them before we stake the sons of bitches," Dallas said solidly.

Vinny, Hunter, and Tito all nodded in agreement.

"How do you plan on drawing them out?" Jones asked curiously.

"You let us worry about that. All I need from you is your cooperation and assistance when we do draw them out. Can I count on you?" Mal asked, sizing up Jones across from him. While he trusted Vinny, life had taught Malcolm that trust wasn't always so easily afforded to strangers, especially in this life.

"Absolutely," Jones said as he raised his glass in response.

"I don't know about you dumbasses but I could use a drink," Dallas said as he got up, nodding at Mal. "You drinking tonight?"

"Does the day end in y? What kind of question is that?" Mal said with a chuckle, rolling his eyes as Dallas took off for the bar.

***

The uproar of laughter was downright infectious as Mal finished his tequila shot.

"I'm telling you, you should have been there. Scared by a fucking raccoon!" Hunter slapped his hand on the table.

BLOOD OF MY ENEMY

Jones drained the rest of his shot as he leaned back against the wall.

The jukebox queued up its next song, but the bar was anything but quiet in between songs. In fact, the chatter itself was loud enough that Mal could have considered it a melody of its own. The notes of Ted Nugent's *Stranglehold* filled the air a moment later as Mal made his way up toward the bar, ready to grab another round.

He pushed through the crowd at the bar, sidling up to the last barstool, next to a woman who looked to be lost in thought. She stirred her cocktail straw in her glass absentmindedly, and as she did so, Malcolm felt the strangest feeling wash over him; almost like a sense of peace or tranquility. But perhaps, that was the alcohol speaking.

ARIEL DAWN

"Can I buy you a drink?" he shouted over the chatter and music. She turned her head, and Mal couldn't help but be struck by her features.

Bright, bluish-green eyes stood out against the dark teal eye shadow she wore. Her long, thick hair fell over her shoulders in deep bronze waves, a few braids woven in between the curls and wispy feathers. She wore a caramel, leather, fringed jacket, the strands of beaded necklaces clanking together as she shifted in her seat. Her gaze roved over him, and he felt strangely seen, almost as if this woman could see through him down to his very soul.

"You're not from around here," she said sweetly, biting her lip.

Mal could feel his cock stirring at the sight. "Just passing through," he said as he held up his hand, signaling the bartender. "What are you drinking?" he asked, nodding to her drink.

Her eyes perked up, her smile lifting just the slightest. "Fuzzy navel," she said with a giggle.

Mal let out a laugh of his own. "Never been a fan of peaches, but whatever the lady wants."

The bartender finally made his way over to them, and Mal rattled off his order rather quickly, before turning back to the woman.

"As I was saying, whatever the lady wants, she gets," he said with a wink.

"What's your name, stranger?" she asked as she scooted her barstool closer, her eyes twinkling with curiosity.

"Malcolm, but everyone calls me Mal."

The woman giggled once more, the

ARIEL DAWN

motion making her necklaces and bracelets jingle and clank. The lights of the bar caught in the silver, copper, and gold bangles on her wrist, refracting the light like tiny dancing pixies on the walls.

"Well, *Mal,* it's a pleasure to meet you, I'm Clementine, but most people call me Cleo."

"Well, that's not a name you hear every day," he said as he shifted his stance. To his surprise, she did the same, the motion bringing them closer. Close enough that her legs brushed his, causing his blood to heat, his pulse to race, and his cock to twitch once more.

"Well, *Malcolm,* I'm not the kind of girl you meet every day," she said with a twist of her lips.

A smile tugged at his own lips and he

nodded to the dance floor. "Care for a dance, my darling Clementine?" he asked as he darted his tongue out, licking his suddenly dry lips.

Before she could even speak, the bartender delivered the round of shots and a fuzzy navel. Mal shook his head, the trancelike state he'd been in evaporating for the moment.

"I believe this is yours," he said as he pushed the small drink toward her, but he did not let go, his fingers wrapping around the cold glass.

Time stood still and moved quickly all at once as Cleo glanced down at his fingertips while she slowly reached out and touched his hand, her skin soft, smooth. The moment in which they touched seemed to go on forever but was over far too soon as she pulled the glass from his hand, bringing it up to her lips.

"Thanks," she said as she gazed up through her long eyelashes at him.

Mal nodded. "I, uh, need to drop these off..." he started, finding it hard to speak for the moment.

The strangest feeling overcame him, as if being away from her... as if it would *hurt.*

He pulled his hand back, shaking his head again.

What the hell is in these shots?

With his newfound clarity, he grabbed the tiny shot glasses in his hands and headed back to the table.

6

CLEO FOUGHT TO control her breath. Her heart raced and her body flushed with heat.

Heat.

She'd heard the stories, but they didn't do it justice, no. From the moment he came close, she knew.

She knew this stranger, this *Malcolm,* was the one.

Everything in the room stilled, all

noise ceased, except for the sound of his heartbeat thumping away in his chest.

The rush of blood in his veins.

His breath.

The animal inside of her *stirred*.

No, it awakened.

And that was just what had happened when he slid next to her at the bar.

Rocky had gone off to take a phone call. Though, she wasn't clear if it was his parents or perhaps one of his brothers. She'd only nodded when he motioned he was going outside and left with her fuzzy navel to enjoy the sights of Howlers tonight.

The need to shift was overwhelming. The music, which had been quiet before to her ears was suddenly very loud, the chatter amongst the townsfolk just as

ARIEL DAWN

blaring. The lights were too bright, and Cleo closed her eyes, trying to adjust. It was like the world was spinning.

"Cleo, are you—" Rocky's voice changed from the normal, even tone to that of something else.

Something darker, edgier.

"Yes," she breathed, feeling the weight of her words.

"Who?" Rocky asked, his voice catching in his throat.

She forced her eyes open, needing to see the expression on his face. His eyes sparkled, flecks of gold shimmering in his deep-green irises, and the look on his face was both hungry and pained.

Cleo's gaze darted around the room, searching for Malcolm, the man who'd done the impossible.

The man who stirred the heat within

BLOOD OF MY ENEMY

her.

Soon enough, she'd transition; it was only a matter of time. The thought terrified her, but she couldn't think about such things, right now. Not when she noticed she was getting some strange looks from some of the inhabitants.

From the other *werewolves*.

Looks that sent chills up her spine, throwing her awakened wolf a new curveball.

Malcolm was nowhere to be found in the crowd. Like a phantom, he had disappeared, leaving her like *this*.

"I—"

"Another werewolf?" Rocky asked with concern.

Cleo shook her head. "I don't think so. I think... I think he was just a regular mortal. Not... one of us..." she answered as the heat kept coming in droves, like an endless string of hot flashes.

Cleo pressed her legs tightly together as the heat made its way through her body, settling in her stomach and her groin. The *need* she felt was something of its own volition, like a being or entity trapped within her frame, begging to come out.

Begging to *hunt* down the one who had awakened her wolf.

"Why are they looking at me like that?" she asked feeling the weight of their gazes.

Rocky let out a deep sigh. "Don't look at them," he directed, grabbing her by the wrist. "We need to get out of here."

She could feel the sweat starting to

form on the small of her back, her temperature starting to rise.

She nodded as she gripped Rocky's wrist as he pulled her close, wrapping his free arm around her back. This close to him she could smell his sweet scent—like vanilla and freshly brewed tea. She could also feel his rigid erection pressing against her thigh, something that both intrigued her but also alarmed her.

"Rocky—" she started to speak, wanting to explain, but her words were interrupted when she heard a familiar voice ringing through the air. She didn't even have to look to know who it belonged to. After all, the voice of an alpha was indistinguishable. Alaric's voice boomed over the rest of the crowd, and just as her eyes met Sawyer's, Rocky spoke.

ARIEL DAWN

"Kiss me."

"What?" Cleo's eyes widened in surprise, taken aback by his comment.

"You're giving off pheromones right now that tell me and every other wolf in this bar that you're in heat. You really want to explain to my brother, the man you're supposed to—" Rocky's voice caught in his throat, unable to speak aloud what they both knew "That a *human* is responsible?"

The reality of his words hit her like a ton of bricks. Rocky was right. At least if she kissed him, made enough of a scene, the surrounding vultures would think Rocky had stirred her heat. They would think he had a claim on her.

"Kiss me," Rocky commanded again as Sawyer and Alaric made their way through the crowd, heading directly

BLOOD OF MY ENEMY

toward them.

Cleo didn't waste another moment as she turned to Rocky, snaking her fingers into his soft, light-brown hair, and crushing her lips against his.

7

"ROCKY? WHAT THE hell?" Alaric's voice boomed as his dark eyes settled on Cleo. "You're not supposed to be here..." Alaric slid his hand between them, just as their lips parted.

Her eyes met Sawyer's, and in them, she could see the fire of a thousand suns.

"Alaric, she's—"

Alaric's nose twitched as he looked

between her and Rocky, reality hitting him.

"You..." Alaric growled out as he shoved Rocky up against the bar.

"Don't hurt him," Cleo said as she grabbed at Alaric's arm, her hand small against his thick, muscled bicep.

Is it just me, or did he get bigger somehow in the last day?

"Come on, man, let's not do this here, not now... There could be vamps... We can't expose ourselves..." Sawyer said as he came up behind Cleo, his voice steady.

The heat from his proximity warmed her, and her wolf was well aware of the beta in her presence. Though the heat within her swirled like a hurricane, the wolf inside begging to come out. She pushed it down for the moment, still

ARIEL DAWN

trying to understand everything that had just transpired.

It was almost as if the world around her was spinning. Every nerve, every muscle in her body *ached* for relief, relief that she knew could only really be satisfied by one person.

Her mate.

Malcolm.

It had always been understood that an omega's role was to provide the alpha of the pack—and in some cases, the beta as well—with heirs. The Oracle was able to discern the right alpha, or the right pack, the ones who would stir the heat within the omega, who would ultimately bond with her. In some cases, the wolf who stirred an omega's heat would differ from the alpha she would undoubtedly mate with. It wasn't common, but it did happen, though Cleo didn't know of any similar predicaments, least of all not one involving a human.

A human I'll probably never see again.

Rocky was right, I can't tell Alaric the truth.

Alaric growled, his gaze focused on the youngest Thorne.

"You disobeyed the pack order." His voice was low, low enough that only the four of them could hear him.

Something in Cleo clicked, almost as if a switch was turned. She grabbed Alaric by the arm once more, this time with a burst of strength she didn't know she had. "Alaric! Let him go!" She pulled hard, and the lumbering alpha swayed, but it did not do much.

Instead, he cast her an angry glare. "I'll deal with you later, *Cleo*," he snarled, and Cleo couldn't help that the hair on the back of her neck rose, that his ferocity sent a shiver down her spine... and directly to her groin.

This is not the time, heat!

Rocky grabbed for his brother's wrist, trying to remove his hand from his throat.

"Sawyer, take Cleo home," Rocky commanded through stifled breaths.

Alaric tightened his grip, leaning Rocky over the bar, knocking over Cleo's untouched fuzzy navel.

Sawyer wrapped his hand around Cleo's wrist, tugging gently. "Come on, sweetheart," he drawled.

But Cleo did not move. A startling feeling nagged at her as her gaze fell on Rocky, protectiveness swelling her chest toward the man who had risked the wrath of his brothers, of his parents, to sneak her out of the house. Who dared to cover for her, so she would not be ostracized, kicked out, or worse, for going into a heat with someone not even within their own species.

"You do not command my beta! You think because you stirred her heat that you get to be top dog now, huh? That she's yours?" Alaric's lips pulled back in a snarl, and as the bartender came over, he shot him a dirty look. The bartender turned right around, walking the other way. Hoots and hollers from the patrons among chants of "fight" drowned out the music.

"She is *mine*, and nothing can change that," Alaric bit out.

The words hung in the air, her ears buzzing, and her entire body conflicted over everything.

There was no way out.

Heat or no heat, Clementine Srirocco belonged to the Thorne Pack, to their alpha.

Alaric.

Everything converged on her at once and it was too much. The overwhelming desire to run, to shift and flee was prevalent for Cleo, but the desire was not hers entirely, no. For the wolf that had awakened inside of her felt a strange sort of contentedness at Alaric's words.

Alaric had laid claim to her in that moment, and while her wolf understood such things, Cleo could not submit that easily, and she would not.

Not when her true mate was out there, not when the alpha in question was hurting his very own blood because he was a jealous, brooding asshole.

"Alaric Thorne! You listen to me right now!" she shouted, lunging for him once more. Her grip on his arm was tighter this time, and a burst of adrenaline coursed through her, her wolf lunging forward beneath her flesh and blood. Shifting energy coursed through her like an electric shock, and Cleo felt an unnatural aggression bubbling underneath.

Alaric dropped Rocky, who was now catching his breath. Alaric turned to her, looming over her like the animal he truly was.

He cocked his head to the side, his eyes gleaming with flecks of gold light, the mark of a werewolf. His shifting energy held at bay.

"I said, I will deal with you later,"

ARIEL DAWN

Alaric growled darkly as he advanced on her. His hand grasped her by the waist, harshly, drawing her close. The touch was possessive and brutal, which only stirred her wolf's inner anger more.

Cleo froze in his grasp, feeling like a powder keg ready to blow. Though the swirling in her stomach was much more of a flutter and she hated that it was. She hated that her heart, her mind, and her libido seemed to be at warring ends.

Alaric brought his face down, drawing his nose up her neck, past her ear, and into her hair as he breathed deep.

The motion was predatory, but Cleo couldn't deny that it felt... *good*. The wolf inside her agreed, taking over for the moment. She fell forward, into his space, like a lamb ripe for slaughter.

"You need to shift," he whispered in

BLOOD OF MY ENEMY

her ear.

The feel of his breath on her skin made her entire body twitch. "Please don't hurt him," she whispered back, her fingers twisting in his gray shirt. "He didn't do anything wrong, he—"

She wanted to tell the truth. Tell Alaric it was not Rocky who stirred her heat. That Rocky was innocent. But a deep, dark understanding inside of her told her doing so would put Malcolm at risk, and if there was one thing her mind, body, and soul could all agree on, it was that the protection of her mate came before anything else. Like an unwritten rule, an invisible force, she could not say the words.

In that moment, Cleo vowed she would do whatever it took to find *Mal*. Even if it meant going up against Alaric when the time came.

"Go with Sawyer. Shift. We will discuss this at home." His voice was less of a whisper now, but the command was still evident.

Cleo hated that the wolf inside of her submitted to his request, not because she wanted to, but because it was natural, ingrained in her being. Because at the base of all things, she was not an alpha or an adversary.

She was an omega.

His omega.

The future mother of their children.

Though, the thought of breeding with Alaric at the moment was quite conflicting and only agitated her wolf more.

He is right, I need to shift.

I need to transition.

BLOOD OF MY ENEMY

Perhaps then, I'll be able to think clearly again.

Sawyer tugged her wrist again, and this time she followed. Her gaze settled on Rocky, who was rubbing his jaw, but when their eyes met, he nodded in agreement.

What was done was done.

Understanding started to settle, and though every bone in her body wanted to argue, wanted to fight with him on his *command*, she knew Alaric was right. She could feel the desire, the *need*, to shift and transition within her like an undulating current.

A beckoned call to the spirit within her.

And so, she followed Sawyer outside of Howlers into the woods, and gave herself over to the animal inside without question, letting the moonlight bathe her in her truth.

The shift was not painful. It was not as disorienting as it should have been, either. Instead, it felt undeniably right. The soft earth between her paws, the wind rustling against her fur.

Sawyer ran alongside her, nipping at her tail, and it was like she was someone else.

No, *something* else.

She was free.

A creature of blood and bone, of flesh and fur.

And she was so very hungry.

8

DALLAS SLID INTO the driver's seat as Mal folded himself into the passenger's side.

"You know, one of these days you're going to have to drive my ass back to base," Dallas grumbled.

"I'm fine, you are just overreacting," Mal said gruffly.

Dallas chortled. "Yeah, and I'm the Queen of England."

BLOOD OF MY ENEMY

"What's your problem lately, D? Since when did you become such a responsible fucking adult?"

Dallas pulled out onto the shadowed road, heading back toward the Moonflower Motel. "I've always been a responsible adult," he bit back. "I'm the most responsible *adult* in this fucking band, I'll have you know."

"Just because you were married once doesn't mean you're responsible," Mal said without thinking, regretting the words the moment they came out of his mouth. "Fuck, Dallas, I'm sorry. I—"

Dallas sighed, as he reached to turn the radio on. There were two things Dallas didn't talk about. His life before hunting and those he lost.

His wife.

His unborn child.

ARIEL DAWN

The sounds of *Born to Be Wild* filled the car as Dallas focused his gaze through the windshield, his fingers tightening around the steering wheel. Dallas steered them toward the woods and away from the center hub of the town. The Moonflower Motel was not the only hotel in the area, but it wasn't quite as close as the other hotels to the sleepy little town.

Mal focused on the blurring of the dark trees out of the window, figuring it was best to keep his mouth shut at the moment to avoid more dumb shit coming out of his mouth.

To his surprise, Dallas spoke up. "While you were flirting with that girl at the bar, Ava texted me." The way he spoke was solid, unwavering.

Almost as if he was nervous.

BLOOD OF MY ENEMY

Weird.

"Yeah, and?" Mal said as he turned to look at Dallas.

"She should be here by morning." Dallas palmed the steering wheel, turning down the long, dark road. The lights of the town had disappeared now, in the rearview, and all there was, was the long, winding road flanked by the forest on either side. Moonlight shone through the trees, the only light in the darkness.

"I can stay with Vinny if you want."

"What? No, you're not staying with Vinny." Mal shook his head. The last time he'd roomed with Vinny, they'd ended up paying damages to the hotel. As well as they all worked together when it came to the hunt, when they had one goal to work toward, Dallas was great.

ARIEL DAWN

As back up, as a front man for their band, Blood Of My Enemy, and as a knowledgeable fellow hunter, even a trainer. But as a person, Dallas was difficult. He needed freedom. Freedom to disappear whenever he desired, freedom to do as he wished.

Vincent Taylor was the polar opposite. Vinny required order, structure, and needed to know the plans at all times. It was one of the things Mal appreciated most about him. His attention to detail.

Just as he appreciated Dallas's talents. Yet, if he was being honest, he understood Dallas's need for freedom. How certain places, things, and feelings could make him feel stifled, could make him feel boxed in and trapped.

Because Malcolm felt those things as

well, which was probably why rooming with Dallas was a piece of cake. Neither of them asked any questions, and instead, just understood the needs of the other in a way no one else could.

"So you want *her* to stay with Vinny, then?" Dallas said, his voice carrying something Mal couldn't quite pinpoint.

It kind of sounded like jealousy, but why would Dallas be jealous of Vinny? That didn't seem right, so he shrugged it off.

Maybe I'm just off because of that weird feeling from earlier...

"Well, yeah. She gets along with Vinny pretty well," Mal said nonchalantly.

"You're comfortable with him sharing a room with her?" Dallas pressed.

"Yeah, why aren't you? It's not like

there's anything going on between them. Men and women *can* share hotel rooms you know. It's the twenty-first century, D," Mal pointedly joked, but Dallas wasn't laughing.

Before Dallas could answer, the headlights shone on a large, brown-furred creature, its golden eyes ghostlike in the gleam, and Mal hollered, "Dallas, watch out!"

Dallas swerved hard to avoid the creature but was not successful. The thud of its body hitting the car was unmistakable, and Dallas slammed on the brakes, throwing Malcolm forward in his seat.

"Fuck!" Mal said as he braced himself against the dashboard.

Dallas scrambled out of the car as Mal followed.

BLOOD OF MY ENEMY

They approached the creature, the... *wolf.*

Only, as Malcolm set his gaze on the large body, he could not help but feel a twinge of fear.

He'd seen plenty of wolves in his time, but this... this was different. It resembled a wolf in every aspect—but it was *huge.* Its paws were larger than any wolf he'd ever seen, its head nearly the size of a prize pumpkin.

The creature's body rose and fell, and he could see blood. Blood on the wolf, blood on his sterling headlight frames, spattered against the bright red paint of his car, and it wasn't crimson like most animal blood. It was darker, almost black.

Dallas kneeled next to the creature to assess its state. Growling could be heard

ARIEL DAWN

in the distance, and as Malcolm turned to the sound, he was taken aback by a force of nature, making her way through the woods, stumbling on bare legs and feet onto the asphalt, a look of abject terror in her eyes.

He braced his arms around hers, holding her still, noticing she was naked.

Naked and... *bleeding.*

Blood trickled down her neck, down her arms, but he wasn't certain if it was her blood or—

"It's all right, Miss, let me help you..." he said as he held her steady. When she looked up, he was met with familiar green-blue eyes, and his heart felt as if it would cease to work. A shiver ran down his spine, his throat going dry, and that strange magnetic pull was back.

"Cleo?" he asked in surprise.

BLOOD OF MY ENEMY

She looked up at him, her eyes dancing with alarm. "Malcolm..." she whispered, her voice barely audible.

Before he could speak, before he could answer her, her eyes fluttered closed, and her body went limp. He caught her, lifting her in his arms, and just as he turned to Dallas, he saw several glowing eyes on the edge of the forest, several pairs of long, perfectly white teeth, accompanied by deep, feral growls.

"Dallas, we need to get out of here," he said as the hair on his neck rose.

"Affirmative, Ghost Rider," Dallas echoed as he stood once more, shaking his head.

"Put her in the backseat, let's go," he commanded.

Malcolm didn't question his directive,

ARIEL DAWN

doing as he said.

It was only moments until they'd both piled in the car, and Dallas was starting the ignition. Malcolm could see the wolves in the rearview mirror advancing on them.

"We gotta go, man..." he said as his nerves stood at attention. Something about these wolves seemed... off. But he couldn't place his finger on it.

"Where's the closest hospital?" Dallas asked as Mal slammed the dashboard. Dallas whipped the car into reverse, jostling them all.

Cleo groaned in the back seat, pain evident in her voice.

"No hospital," she coughed out.

"What? Are you insane? You're hurt. You—"

"No. Hospital," she said much clearer.

BLOOD OF MY ENEMY

"I don't like this, Mal," Dallas said, his voice raising an octave.

"I'll be... fine," she said, trying to sit up.

"No," Mal said, his voice ringing in the air.

"Don't move, just... rest. We'll... we'll figure something out."

Dallas huffed in annoyance, the steering wheel squeaking from his grip.

"I hope you have a plan, then," he gritted out through his teeth as they made their way to the Moonflower Motel with a rather unexpected guest.

9

CLEO HAD NEVER felt more free. The world was her oyster when she was in her true form. Sawyer led her through the woods, toward her first kill. She watched him intently, studying his movements, learning quickly. Combined with the instincts of the animal inside her, who was now front and center, it was a piece of cake.

Then again, she'd always been a fast

BLOOD OF MY ENEMY

learner.

Blood filled her mouth; the warm, sticky liquid sliding down her throat was *divine*. The crunch of bone and muscle was like music to her ears, and she wanted more.

More of everything.

In this form, her senses were heightened. It was simple. When she'd had her fill of her first kill, she tilted her head back and howled at the moon. Sawyer answered her call, coming up beside her and throwing his head back as well. Cleo felt regal, as if nothing could stop her, as if everything was the way it should be for the moment. A nudge from Sawyer diverted her attention. He nodded in the direction of deeper wood, and her wolf understood without question.

ARIEL DAWN

He wanted to run.

And so they ran.

In the darkness that swallowed them, there was only the chase. The hunt.

Sawyer nipped at her tail playfully, and she picked up the pace. Nearing out of breath due to not being used to this form, she stopped suddenly. It was only a minuscule moment before Sawyer playfully pounced on her, knocking her over.

The cool earth against her fur was a welcome feeling, and strangely, so was the feeling of his heavy form mounting her. In his golden eyes, she could see they were wild with excitement, almost glowing of their own accord, and the sight spoke to her wolf in a way she could have never comprehended if someone had told her.

BLOOD OF MY ENEMY

And they had.

Many times.

She knew everything that being born an omega would entail for her one day, but now that the day was here, it was all so confusing, so baffling trying to make sense of it all.

The heat returned, flooding her body with thoughts, emotions, and desires that were completely foreign to her. She wanted this, that she knew, but it wasn't Sawyer she wanted.

Not really.

Though her wolf did not seem to mind Sawyer in this form, Cleo knew it was too soon. Just as Sawyer bit at her neck, as he pressed himself closer, lining himself up, an unmistakable scent filled the air.

Sawyer paused, turning his head. He

could smell it, too. She was certain.

Cleo rose, pushing him off of her, the both of them righting themselves, their haunches rising.

The smell of death was unmistakable.

In all her years being raised across the ridge, Cleo had never smelled the blood of her enemies.

Vampires.

She'd been told vampires didn't come that way. They knew better than to cross into werewolf territory.

But those days were gone. When the vampires came, no one was prepared.

Why they came, she wasn't certain, but she had been lucky. Lucky that leave had been arranged for her, that she was to be delivered to the Thornes.

Though she still felt guilty that all those werewolves were captured or slaughtered in her absence, and here she was now, frolicking in the woods with the beta of her new pack, moments away from making a decision that would tie her to Sawyer for the rest of her life, a decision which would undoubtedly anger her alpha, the man she was supposed to mate with.

I need to find Malcolm.

Before Sawyer and Cleo could disperse, they came through the woods, to the clearing, and their eyes met.

The vampires were a trio; a woman with two males. They all bore the same look, much like shifters did. All three of them pale with striking features. The woman was frighteningly beautiful, with ice-blue eyes and long, jet-black hair. The smile on her face was somewhat unhinged, the blood dripping down her chin only adding to the aesthetic.

The two men that flanked her were of average build. One had similar features; his black hair slicked back, the oil shining in the moonlight. His eyes were dark like the night. And the last was a man with copper hair, his eyes a darker shade of blue than the lady vampire's.

"Well, well, darlings, look what we have here." She bit her lip in anticipation.

Cleo growled instinctively, the animal inside of her waiting with bated breath to lunge for the wicked monster.

Sawyer was beside her, snarling in warning as saliva dripped down his fangs over his jaw into a puddle on the ground.

One of the men sniffed the air.

"The white one is in heat, Edie."

BLOOD OF MY ENEMY

Before the woman, before this *Edie,* could speak, Cleo felt the presence of another wolf.

Two wolves in fact.

She didn't even have to wonder who they were. They smelled like Sawyer, for one, and her wolf immediately recognized the scent and presence of her alpha.

The black wolf flanked the largest. Cleo knew without asking which they were. Alaric and Rocky growled ferociously as Alaric stepped in front of her.

"I told you, Robert, no one calls me Edie. It is *Eden* or *my queen* to you."

Cleo watched as Eden turned to her vampire ally, wrapping her fingers around his throat, startling the man. The other vampire looked unbothered, uninterested in the happenings. Perhaps this was normal behavior for vampires. After all, they were vicious, bloodsucking leeches.

Eden withdrew her hand as she locked eyes with Cleo.

"Look how they protect her. Loyal to their pack, darling."

Alaric lunged forward, Sawyer and Rocky on either side of her now.

A wicked giggle escaped Eden's throat.

"Oh, do you really think you are a match for a *queen*, pup?" She rolled her eyes as she advanced on Alaric.

Cleo watched, frozen as Eden's eyes started to glow an almost iridescent shade of lilac.

She could see Alaric's legs shaking, as if he was trying to move, but something was preventing him from doing so.

He whined and growled, snapping his jaw.

"Bring me the omega," she said as she tilted her head, just as Alaric fell to the ground with a yelp.

It was a blur after that. Sawyer and Rocky lunged forward, and Cleo did not wait to descend, snapping her jaws at the vampires as Eden bared her fangs back. Alaric was down for the count, his body rising and falling, the only indication he was alive.

When hands wrapped themselves around her middle, Cleo used every ounce of strength she had to overthrow the black-haired vampire, but it was too late.

Fangs sunk into her furry flesh, and

ARIEL DAWN

she felt as if her entire being was being burned alive. She howled in pain as Sawyer attacked from the side, pushing the vampire down. Rocky nudged her, taking off like a bat out of hell, and she knew without question, what she needed to do.

She needed to run, to shift.

To get as far away from the vampires and the woods as possible.

It was a strange form of understanding, that she and her pack could communicate such things without words. With just a look at Rocky's glowing eyes, she knew he would lead her out of the darkness into safety.

Just as he had kept her secret to keep her safe.

Because that was who Rocky Thorne was.

BLOOD OF MY ENEMY

A safe haven.

She ran as fast as she could, and this time, shifting came much faster. Her bones snapped and cracked back into shape, until, within moments, she was running on bare human feet, naked and bleeding, following the large black wolf to the edge of the woods.

The road came into view, and neither of them saw the car driving a speedy seventy miles an hour.

"Rocky!" she yelled as her black wolf in shining fur was thrust up against the front of a car, the thud of his body hitting the car and pavement a dire sound.

Adrenaline fueled Cleo as she ran toward Rocky. She looked over her bare shoulder at the woods, her heart sinking.

ARIEL DAWN

What if Alaric and Sawyer don't make it, what if—

No, I can't think like that.

I need to save Rocky, need to make sure he's all right.

Cleo's body came up against a solid one, warm hands sliding along her arms as they braced her. Instantly, her entire body felt alive, every nerve, every synapse firing at the touch that felt almost euphoric on her skin. Even if he hadn't spoken, she would have known.

She'd know the touch of her mate anywhere, in any form.

And perhaps that was why, when the adrenaline crashed, when her wolf had finally finished its transition, she felt weak.

As if the darkness could consume her whole.

BLOOD OF MY ENEMY

But in Malcolm's arms, in his car, she knew deep within her bones that he felt it too.

Their bond.

She could feel it like an invisible tether between them, sense his emotion, his own turmoil.

The back of his car was comfortable and smelled like tobacco and whiskey. It was a warm, soothing scent and she wanted very badly to curl up into a ball and fall asleep, the leather of his seats cool against her skin. Her fingers twisted in something soft, almost velvety. Opening her eyes, she saw it was a flannel shirt, and she tugged the fabric closer.

When the driver, a man who Malcolm called *Dallas* suggested they take her to a hospital, she'd said no. That one word

ARIEL DAWN

alerted her, and she knew the rules packs had about trusting humans and human hospitals. She knew she should be wary of the both of them, these humans, but she couldn't find it within herself to distrust them.

Not when one of them was her mate.

Werewolves needed to be kept a secret. The humans could never know they existed, if they did, unspeakable things would happen.

The last thing she remembered before drifting off into sleep in the back of Malcolm's car was the promise he'd made, that somehow, someway they would figure this all out.

10

"WHAT THE FUCK are you thinking?" Dallas growled as he hit his hand against the steering wheel.

Mal glanced at the tiny needle hovering over seventy-five. "Slow down, D."

"Don't fucking tell me to slow down when you have a naked, bleeding woman in the car who you refuse to take to a goddamned hospital," he said as they

BLOOD OF MY ENEMY

turned down the road that would bring them to the Moonflower Motel. "Just what is your plan, huh?" Dallas's face was turning all shades of pink.

Mal's own blood started to boil. "Well, for starters, I think she needs a shower, some clean clothes, and maybe then, we can ask her what the hell happened. Take her home."

Dallas let out a dark laugh. "What is wrong with you? It's like ever since we hit this goddamned town, you've been out of left field," Dallas bit out as he whipped the car into the parking lot, turning it off.

"Me? You're the one who's acting like a fucking pod person!" Mal said as he threw open the door.

"Being the responsible one does not make me a fucking pod person."

ARIEL DAWN

"You're not my fucking father, Dallas. Stop treating me like I'm some punk-ass kid!"

Dallas slammed the driver's side door, yanking open the back passenger door.

"Stop acting like one and grow the fuck up!" he snarled as he wrapped his arms around Cleo.

Mal's blood chilled. "Don't touch her," he said as he came up against Dallas. His mind was swimming, going a hundred miles a minute.

Something felt off.

He felt off.

I haven't even had that much to drink!

Dallas removed his arms from Cleo, and she sunk back into the seat as he then grabbed Malcolm by the shirt.

Mal twisted in his grasp, pushing him

BLOOD OF MY ENEMY

away.

"What do you plan to do, leave her in the car all night?" Dallas growled.

"Get the fuck out of here. I'm not dealing with you right now," Mal said as he pulled Cleo to him, picking her up in his arms.

Dallas shook his head. "Un-fucking-believable."

Cleo's head lolled against his shoulder, the soft, golden edges of her hair brushing against his neck.

"Take a walk, Dallas," Mal directed.

Dallas threw his hands in the air. "My pleasure, Malcolm. Don't come calling me when shit hits the fan and you have blood on your hands."

The use of his full name signified just how pissed Dallas was.

He never used Mal's full name.

ARIEL DAWN

Ever.

In his brain, he knew Dallas was right. He was being irrational, being stupid. But every bone in his body, every fiber of his being knew what she needed. Knew somehow, in some unexplainable way, that this woman, *Clementine*, needed him.

Just like Ava needed him.

Like his parents did.

"Stay with me, Cleo," he whispered as she snaked her arm around his neck, holding on. She wasn't completely asleep, but he could tell she was not in the best shape.

Dallas was right.

She probably needed a hospital.

Yet, Cleo had adamantly spoken against it, and there must be a reason.

A reason he would get to the bottom

of soon enough when she was clean, clothed, and fed.

***

Malcolm waited beside the tub, steam rising from the water in tiny tendrils. He kept his fingers on her pulse, noting it had started to pick up quickly.

Cleo tossed and turned in the water.

In the light of their hotel room, he could see her beauty for what it was. She wasn't pale, but her skin boasted a golden hue to it, a faint bronze as if the sun was responsible. Her hair, which he could see more clearly, a dark brown fading to blonde, with streaks of copper and gold all throughout, stuck to her skin, darkened by the water. It fell over her breasts, covering her nipples, and he had to look away more than once.

ARIEL DAWN

In the bar, it had been difficult to discern her silhouette, but naked in his tub, the swell of her breasts was hard to ignore. They weren't exactly small or mediocre by any means.

"What the fuck am I doing?" he asked aloud.

"Malcolm, is that... is that you?" her voice was small, soft.

Barely audible.

Yet, it stirred something within him he didn't know existed.

Hope.

"Yes," he answered, unsure of what to say or do. He'd never been in a situation quite like this before.

"Where... where are we?" Cleo's eyes fluttered, and he sat up straighter.

"In my hotel room. We... wanted to take you to a hospital but you said no hospitals, so..."

Cleo pulled her knees up to her chest, and upon realization, a maddening blush formed on her cheeks.

"Oh my God. I am—"

Mal handed her a towel, as he turned his head away. "I, um... here."

Her fingers touched his as she pulled the towel away from him, a soft gasp escaping her throat. "Thanks," she said kindly.

He rose from his spot on the cold, tile floor, turning around, his eyes facing the open door. "You don't... need help, do you?" he asked, feeling strangely nervous, as if he'd never been in the same room with a naked woman before.

Which was insane.

He was thirty-one years old. He'd been with plenty of women before.

ARIEL DAWN

So why was this one different?

Why did he feel like everything was so fragile?

Why did he feel that strange magnetic feeling in the pit of his stomach?

"I think I can manage," she answered, and he heard the sloshing of the water as she stood.

"Um, okay. I, um, unfortunately, I don't travel with a lot of clothes, so all I have is a pair of boxers and a shirt. They're clean, though, so..." He swallowed as he headed for the door. "When you're ready, we can talk about what happened." His voice was steady as the words hung in the air.

It seemed like an eternity until Cleo spoke.

"Thank you," she said as he walked through the door, closing it behind him to give her privacy.

When Mal sat on the bed, his shoulders sunk and the tension disintegrated. Adrenaline had coursed through him, and now, he just felt tired.

So very tired.

He looked at the digital clock on the nightstand, noting the time read nearly 11:30 p.m. Running his hand through his hair, he couldn't shake the feeling that something supernatural was afoot. With Dallas gone, the alcohol and adrenaline out of his system, and the beautiful Cleo away from his sight, he could finally think straight.

Malcolm ran the night's events over and over in his head and could only come to one conclusion.

Cleo had been bitten by vampires.

It was the only thing that made

ARIEL DAWN

logical sense, given the blood on her neck and arm, but it didn't explain why she was running naked through the woods, or the oversized, gigantic wolf who had hit his car.

His throat tightened as his thoughts traveled down dark paths.

If the vampires bit her, who was to say they hadn't had their way with her?

The thought caused his blood to heat, anger to flood him. He didn't even notice until she spoke that she had left the bathroom.

"Thank you, for... helping me."

"I didn't do anything," he grumbled, looking away.

Cleo took small steps forward, that magnetic pull getting stronger.

"You didn't run away. You could've left me and Rocky—"

BLOOD OF MY ENEMY

Who is Rocky?

"Who's Rocky?" he asked aloud.

Cleo took another step. "A friend."

Mal turned his head, his gaze finally settling on her. In his black, boxer shorts and white T-shirt, she looked just as stunning, if not more than when he'd first laid eyes on her at the bar. She was shorter than he initially thought, though. Standing before him, she looked to be barely five-foot-three.

"This friend responsible for hurting you?" he asked carefully.

Cleo took a few more steps, now in front of him. She smelled like heaven. Like hotel soap and sweet honey. The magnetic pull was strong, and he couldn't help the desire that somehow felt louder than anything else. The desire to touch her to know she was real. The desire to breathe in her sweet, honey scent and let it fill his airways.

The desire to protect that which was *his.*

Which was crazy because he barely knew this woman, yet, as he looked up at her bright, green-blue eyes, he knew beyond any reasonable explanation this was the truth.

"What are you?" he asked, trying to fight the urge to touch her. To run his hands along her sun-kissed thighs, over her soft skin, to wrap his arms around her and never let go.

The emotion, the thoughts, it was all quite jarring, and he only knew of very few creatures capable of manipulating someone to that extent. But Cleo didn't look like a vampire. She didn't have the telltale signs of a bloodsucker, either.

BLOOD OF MY ENEMY

She was beautiful as sin, but she didn't have the markings of a demon or succubus, which was the first thing he'd checked for when laying her in the tub.

"What?" she asked, her voice shaking.

He reached out, unable to fight the need in this moment. He set his hand on her hip, pulling her closer, gesturing for her to sit beside him. Her skin was soft, warm, and stirred a heat within him that cemented his suspicion Cleo was not as she seemed. He'd been with plenty of women, and no one ever made him feel anything remotely close to this.

"I said, what are you? You're not a vampire, but you've done something to me. Is this part of your trap? Lure unsuspecting men into your web and—"

"No, it's not like that," she said as she followed his lead, sitting next to him.

ARIEL DAWN

"Then tell me, Cleo. What is it like? What kind of monster are you?"

The words out of his mouth were in stark contrast to what he wanted to ask. What he knew he should ask.

If she was attacked by vampires, he needed to know how many there were. How long they'd fed, if one had spread venom...

Was Cleo a ticking time bomb?

Would she become one of them?

What happened when vampires bit other supernaturals?

Did they even do such a thing?

The questions kept mounting, but all he could focus on was her. On her hypnotic, blue-green eyes that reminded him of the ocean. On the way her lips formed a perfect cupid's bow. On her damp hair falling over her shoulder, and how enticing she looked wearing his clothes.

Cleo moved closer to him, and he did not move away, even though he knew he should.

"You wouldn't believe me if I told you," she said as she shifted her weight, leaning on her left leg as she turned to face him.

Instinctually, he reached out, pushing a stray strand of dark hair behind her ear, his gaze settling on her lips. He swallowed nervously before the words fell out of his mouth.

"Try me."

11

THERE WERE PLENTY of times in Cleo's life she'd been alone with a man. She'd had boyfriends, some who she'd even been intimate with, even though such a thing was traditionally frowned upon for omegas. Everyone was always concerned about the heat, and her former lovers were no different; wanting to be the lucky one who stirred such things, wanting to be the one responsible for her transition, to form the bond.

Malcolm's words didn't make sense.

He was a human, what did he know of vampires?

Of monsters?

His words should have been alarming to her, should have been a warning, a red flag.

Was he one of those slayers?

A hunter?

The very thing that forced her kind into hiding because they thought they were monsters?

Every bit of Cleo knew if there was even the sliver of a chance such a thing was true, she should turn tail and run. But instead, she found herself reaching out to him, her fingertips brushing the back of his hand. The cyclone inside her started to rise again, the heat returning with a vengeance.

It was overwhelming.

"I am an omega," she said the words plainly, softly.

Mal cocked his head to the side, a curious look on his face. "A what?"

He moved closer by an inch, and she pretended not to notice. It still felt as if a canyon of space lay between them, despite the fact he was only inches away from her now.

"I believe your kind knows mine as werewolves." Cleo did not miss the look of shock as it registered on Malcolm's face, his eyes widening, his mouth opening in disbelief.

"A werewolf?" he said, deadpan, though he did not remove his hand. His fingers traced her cheek, then moved slowly down her jaw, before he used his thumb to brush over her lips. "Like a wolfman, Van Helsing lycanthrope?" He swallowed, his voice stern.

Cleo nodded. "Yes. I am, you—stirred my heat."

Malcolm froze in place, his brows furrowed. "I did what now?"

"You stirred my heat, in the bar. You are my mate."

He dropped his hand suddenly, and it was as if the words were a splash of cold water. "That's not possible."

Cleo could not take her eyes off of him, and the moment he scrambled away, she felt a dire ache in her heart, in her loins.

The wolf inside her pushed forth.

No...

"It is. There is no mistake. I know you feel it too, I—"

ARIEL DAWN

"I can't believe this," he said as he ran his hand through his hair.

Cleo rose slowly from the bed. "I transitioned. Shifted in the woods for the first time, and then, the vampires came, and it all happened so quickly I—"

Malcolm started to pace back and forth in the small room. "Did one of them bite you?" he asked abruptly.

"Yes."

Mal cursed, his fist hitting the wall.

"They did not drink, though. My pack, they did not give them the chance," she said as the images played back in her mind. "I will heal, I—"

"Why me?" he asked, flustered. He motioned toward her, and she could clearly see he was trying to process it all just as she was. It was a lot to take in.

Even if he was a hunter, he did not

seem to know much about her kind. His surprise at the mention of her heat was proof enough.

"I don't know!" she said, starting to feel her own panic. "I only came to Mahoning three weeks ago on the hope my heat would stir. The Oracle said so! She claimed the Thornes would be responsible! Not a human! This isn't what I asked for, either!"

Anger and sadness culminated in her being, an instinctual fear.

Is he... rejecting me?

Mal let out a deep sigh, his gaze roving over her, and under his gaze, she felt hot. Her wolf paced, feeling agitated at the thought.

"Are you... rejecting this? Rejecting me?" she asked, though the words came out in a much harsher tone than she'd

ARIEL DAWN

wanted.

Mal stood only a few feet away, and in the light of his motel room, she could finally *see* him. He wasn't tall like the Thorne brothers, not as defined in build, either. Instead, he was of average height, toned enough that it looked as if he probably worked out. His dark hair and facial hair coupled with the harsh shadows from the room and his amber eyes made him look inviting as hell, and Cleo couldn't help the swarm of butterflies in her stomach as she looked at him.

As if she'd lost her mind entirely, ruled by nothing else than the animal hijacking her body and brain, she stepped closer, closing the distance between them.

"I don't even know you," he said, his

BLOOD OF MY ENEMY

voice dark.

Cleo's rational brain wanted to agree, but the heat, the animal inside of her did not know rationale. It only knew instinct, and at this very moment, she could not fight the instinct.

So, she leaned forward and kissed him.

To her surprise, Malcolm did not pull away.

Instead, he kissed her back fiercely, his hands settling around her waist, pulling her closer. Fire spread throughout her body, ravaging her like she was nothing more than a forest of brittle trees.

"I don't even know your last name," he whispered against her lips, but he did not let go. In fact, his grip tightened on her, as if he was afraid to let her go.

ARIEL DAWN

"Srirocco," she whispered back as her lips took his again. "My name is Clementine June Srirocco, I'm twenty-six years old, and I am an omega. My favorite color is purple, and I hate pineapple on pizza," she said with a soft giggle.

Malcolm looked at her, his eyes pulling up in the corners, a sexy smile forming on his face. "I was born Malcolm Crowley, descendant of the infamous Aleister Crowley, but I legally changed my name to Reynolds after my slayer parents were killed by vampires. I'm thirty-one years old, my favorite color is black, and pineapple on pizza is the fucking bomb," he said as he pushed his fingers into her hair, twisting and pulling on the soft tendrils as their lips crashed together again.

BLOOD OF MY ENEMY

But this time, Malcolm deepened the kiss.

His tongue probed hers hungrily, almost as if he, too, was starving.

Cleo's fingernails trailed down his arms, his skin cool to the touch in stark contrast to the fire that was her entire being at this moment. His hands settled just above her ass, and she could feel his arousal against her thigh, and the notion made her brain foggy. It was as if she was completely someone else.

Something else.

Cleo ground her hips against Mal, which elicited a deep groan from his throat as his lips broke away from her mouth, and instead, he kissed her jaw slowly. She could not help the moan of ecstasy that escaped her.

His lips on her skin felt too good.

ARIEL DAWN

Too perfect.

"So you don't reject me..." She gulped, searching for air, searching for the words. She needed to hear them if—

A loud banging interrupted the both of them, their muscles tightening. Cleo felt a pang of fear, and her wolf was on alert.

Who dared to come between her and her mate?

"Open the fucking door!" the voice boomed, and Cleo's heart sank.

"Cleo, stay behind me," Malcolm instructed.

All she could do was nod, wanting to stop this moment in time, so the future could not happen. Because the future would bring consequences she wasn't quite ready to face. Not after she had just found her mate, when they had started to initiate the attachment, to cement their bond.

Cleo watched as Mal opened the door, and golden eyes settled on her, a look of fury on Alaric's face.

"I believe you have something that belongs to me," he said, looming over Malcolm.

She watched as Mal's gaze danced around the room before settling back on Alaric, who looked like he was ready to pop a blood vessel.

"Really? I don't see anything here that belongs to you, actually. Think you have the wrong room." His words were solid, pointedly direct.

"Cleo, get in the car," Alaric growled out.

Cleo found herself at a crossroads. Knowing what she should do and feeling torn between such and what she wanted more than anything.

She wanted to stay.

Here, with Malcolm.

She was certain they could figure this all out, he'd promised... but she also knew she didn't belong here, not really. She belonged with her pack. She knew it and her wolf knew it, just as the sun knew to rise and fall each day.

A wolf's place—no, an *omega's place*—was with her pack.

With her alpha.

Malcolm left his post, turning to face her as Cleo walked slowly toward the door. They met halfway, and as she walked forward, her stomach in knots, a gentle hand stopped her. The touch was as loud as all the unspoken words between them as he regarded her eyes seriously. She met his eyes once more, and in them, she could see he was torn, too.

"You don't have to go with him," Mal said sternly.

"I can't stay," she whispered, not taking her gaze off him.

"Is he... like you?" Mal asked, his tongue darting out to lick his dry lips.

Cleo nodded. "He's my alpha, Mal. I have to go."

It seemed an eternity existed between them as Alaric loomed in the distance. She could feel his eyes on her.

"When will I see you again?" Mal whispered.

"I'll find you. You are my mate, I will always be able to find you," she whispered back, and then she walked away.

ARIEL DAWN

One foot in front of the other, it felt as if she was walking on a bed of knives, and when she walked out the door, she hoped that her words to Mal held true.

12

MALCOLM'S HEAD WAS swimming, trying to process everything as he fell onto the bed. The events of the night had gone terribly awry, thrown him for a loop.

Meeting Cleo at the bar.

Dallas acting out of character.

Hitting a werewolf, and finding out the woman he was more than attracted to had... mated him?

BLOOD OF MY ENEMY

Was that the right word?

Mal looked at the clock, which now read quarter to two. With Cleo gone, he felt as if everything was much clearer. He adjusted himself in his jeans, banishing all thoughts of her. Being in her presence altered his judgment. That, he could admit.

Her sweet, honey scent, her vivid, beautiful eyes, her soft skin, the soothing candor of her voice...

Malcolm had been in the presence of many women before, but none of them ever crashed through his walls as quickly as this one had.

Because she's not a woman, Mal.

She's a fucking monster.

You can't trust a monster.

Though he knew what she was, he couldn't entirely agree she was a monster. She hadn't done anything to prove that she was. Instead, she seemed to be a victim.

Beholden to a pack.

An alpha.

Attacked by the very things he hunted.

What if it is all a lie?

I know nothing of werewolves.

For Christ's sake, up until today, I didn't even know they were real!

No hunters I know have seen evidence they were!

What if she's lying... what if?

What if I'm being played, and she's the one responsible for the killings?

The thoughts ran rampant in his brain, delving into a thousand different pathways, and he wasn't certain about any of them.

BLOOD OF MY ENEMY

He ran his hand through his hair, sinking back into the bed, exhaustion overcoming him. He glanced over to the door, wondering where she'd gone, where her... *boyfriend* took her, wondering if he'd just made a grave mistake.

Dallas had not returned, either, and he was worried about his friend, but also, he felt a pang of guilt for how he'd reacted when all Dallas was trying to do was the right thing, or what he thought was the right thing.

He always did.

Whereas Malcolm ran with his gut instinct much of the time, Dallas always acted in everyone's best interest, not just his own. So he slid out his phone and sent out a text.

It's been taken care of.

ARIEL DAWN

He didn't bother to wait for Dallas to text back, knowing whatever was going on with his friend, he needed space to sort it out. Ever since the events of Terror Con, it was plain for Malcolm to see his friend was struggling with his own inner demons. Perhaps, he'd gone back to Howlers with the others, to drown himself in drink and tail, and found someone to go home with, someone to make him forget about all his troubles and this fucked-up life they all lived for just a while.

It certainly wouldn't be the first time.

The thought bothered him more than it should, for up until this point, Mal had done the same thing.

It never bothered him before, why should it now?

He refused to answer his own

question, and instead crawled beneath the covers, closed his eyes, and let the darkness consume him.

***

Malcolm awoke to the sound of the door opening.

Dallas must finally be back from whatever bed he landed in last night.

"Rise and shine, Sleeping Beauty."

The voice was unmistakable, and Malcolm immediately groaned as the bed shook once Ava dove onto it next to him, shoving him with her hand.

"Fuck off, Ava."

"Awww, missed you, too," she chimed with another shove.

Mal pushed her away as he sat up in bed, running both his hands over his face and letting his eyes adjust to the

ARIEL DAWN

world once again.

Dallas closed the door behind him, walking in quietly.

"Rough night?" she said, her voice tinged with that permanent sarcasm that seemed to be a Crowley trait. Their mother had the same bite every time she spoke, despite being one of the kindest people on the planet.

"When did you get in?" Mal asked as he avoided her question, reaching for his phone.

"Around two in the morning."

"Shit, that was fast, you must have been going NASCAR the whole way here," Mal said as he threw his legs over the bed.

"Well, I made good time. No detours and nobody on the road that late, so I was lucky." She leaned back against the headboard, pulling her knees up to her chest, and Dallas stood at the foot of his bed, watching the two of them.

"You in a better mood this morning, creeper?" Mal grumbled, nodding at Dallas.

"Sure," Dallas said as he crossed his arms, his face as emotionless as his words.

Mal shrugged as he got out of bed, heading for the bathroom.

The door didn't shut completely, which made it easier to talk, but kept him hidden enough he could pee in peace.

"Where's the girl?" Dallas asked, cutting to the chase.

"Girl?" Ava asked in surprise.

"Mal—"

"I don't need the details, thank you

very much," Ava bristled.

"She went home," Mal called out from the bathroom, the word *home* echoing in the bathroom like some sort of omen.

"Oh my God, you didn't like... fuck her on this bed, did you?" Ava shouted in disgust.

He could hear her practically jumping off the bed and the notion made him smile, a laugh forming in his throat. "Wouldn't you like to know," he taunted as he finished up, washing his hands.

"You are disgusting!" she hollered back.

When he came out of the bathroom, he was face-to-face with Dallas.

"What happened?" he pressed.

Mal moved around him. "I told you, she went home," Mal said, wanting nothing more than to avoid this conversation. Though, he knew he should be truthful and tell Dallas they had more than vampires to worry about, his stomach sunk at the thought.

How could he expose Cleo like that?

His... *mate?*

No.

You need to get a hold of yourself, Mal.

She's not anything to you.

She's not even human.

Though, as he thought the words, he knew they were a lie, and he hated that. So instead, he led with what he did know. "She got cleaned up, I lent her some of my clothes, and she told me she was attacked by vamps."

"So they are here for sure, then," Ava said with a smile.

Mal nodded. "Yup. One bit her, but

he didn't drink. Some wolves showed up, attacked the bastards, and she got away."

Dallas sat on the edge of the bed, leaning his chin on his palm. "Anything else?" He raised his eyebrow.

How Dallas knew he was withholding information was something he normally admired, but today he was skeptical...

Though he trusted Dallas, he wasn't sure he wanted to disclose everything about his meeting with Cleo, not until he had more answers, and certainly not in front of his sister. His gaze wandered to Ava's wrist, her bite mark scar shimmering in the streams of morning light pouring in through the blinds.

"Nope. Bite mark was already starting to heal since they didn't drink, and no venom was spread... no claim made.

BLOOD OF MY ENEMY

She... called her boyfriend, he came and got her. End of story." Malcolm turned away, heading for his duffel bag to find some jeans and a clean shirt.

"Doesn't explain why she was in the woods. Naked," Dallas pressed again.

"Pretty self-explanatory, D, you know how vamps like to prey on innocent girls." His words were harsher than he meant as his gaze traveled to his sister, who had shifted closer to where Dallas sat. They both looked at him in question, like some nightmarish version of Starsky and Hutch.

"What was she doing in the woods?" Ava asked inquisitively.

Mal bit his tongue, silently cursing. Of course his sister would ask questions when he didn't have answers to give. Not only did he not want to answer her, he

ARIEL DAWN

didn't want to think about the implications at all, either.

The thought of Cleo shifting into a creature like the one he'd hit...

"Probably just went for a walk. Wrong place, wrong time," he said as he pulled on his favorite Metallica shirt.

It was then, at that moment, Malcolm realized Ava had mentioned she'd gotten in mere hours ago. He looked at the clock, which read eight in the morning.

She'd been in town for six hours, and she'd waited until *now* to show up?

Where was she?

Panic coursed through him as the thought of her wandering alone in a town riddled with werewolves and vampires pushed to the front of his mind.

"So why didn't you show up here

when you got in? You know, six hours ago?" Mal diverted, his voice tinged in alarm as he led the line of conversation away from Cleo, and all thoughts of how she felt close against him, of how sweet she tasted, and how, even now, he felt empty, hollow away from her.

Fucking hell...

There's got to be a way out of this.

Ava's facial expression did not falter; poker face as usual.

"In my room, tucked in bed like a good little girl." She winked at him, a sly smile spreading across her lips.

Dallas coughed deeply, almost as if he was choking on something as he shifted his weight on the edge of the bed, as if he was uncomfortable for some reason.

Mal raised an eyebrow. "Please. We

ARIEL DAWN

all know you're the furthest thing from *good* in any stretch of the word," he joked. "But seriously, now isn't the time to be off making bad decisions. I think... I think we might have some other creatures in our midst, but I'm not entirely sure."

Dallas perked up. "You mean you agree with Vinny and Jones? That there's something else other than vampires in this small town tearing up bodies?"

Mal nodded slowly, looking at Ava. "Yeah, so forgive me for being a little worried about you coming on this trip, Simba."

Ava sighed, shrugging her shoulders.

"I can handle myself, Mal. You know that. I've held my own against more than just vampires," she said solidly.

BLOOD OF MY ENEMY

The pressure in the room suddenly felt constricting as her words hung in the air. Dallas let out a dissatisfied grunt, and Mal crossed his arms, raising an eyebrow at her.

"But if it makes you feel better, seriously, I texted Dallas, met up with everyone at Howlers, and Vinny offered me up his room. Said he'd stay with Jones while we were all in town, and after we left, he gave me the key. Said he'd be by today to get his stuff sometime. I was pretty exhausted from the drive and a couple drinks before the place closed—"

"A couple? That's putting it mildly," Dallas chimed in, a smirk on his face.

"Sorry, Dad, I promise I won't drink the boys under the table again. Scouts Honor," she said with a wicked laugh,

ARIEL DAWN

and Mal actually couldn't help letting out a laugh himself, especially when he saw how uncomfortable and pissed off Dallas looked from the comment. Not many people were capable of getting under Dallas's skin quite like his sister could. Then again, that was on par for Ava.

She had a way of getting under *everyone's* skin in one way or another, it was just who she was, and if he was being entirely honest, it was one of the qualities they shared.

"One of these days, that mouth is going to get you in a lot of trouble," Dallas grumbled.

"Good thing trouble's my middle name." Ava smiled smugly as Mal rolled his eyes. "As I was saying before Dallas rudely interrupted me, Dallas gave me a lift back and we both pretty much just passed out."

Mal nodded. "Well, I'm glad you got in okay," he said as he started for the door. "Should we collect the others for breakfast or just leave them to their hangovers in peace?" Mal asked as he opened the door.

Sunlight poured in through opening, shining on Dallas, who looked frozen in place like a statue as Ava stood next to him.

"I don't know about you, but I could go for some fucking donuts. Please tell me they have donuts here."

"Well, all I saw was a diner on the way in, so chances are fifty-fifty," Mal said as he turned around and exited, Ava's footsteps loud behind him.

13

"WHAT THE HELL were you thinking?" Alaric said as he smacked his palm against the steering wheel.

Cleo shrunk in the passenger seat, bringing her knees up to her chest. "I don't know, I just... ran. My wolf took over."

"You ran right into the arms of a fucking *hunter*, Cleo."

"You can't keep me locked up in a

tower like some princess, Alaric. Besides, how do you know he's a hunter? He could just be a random traveler, passing through—"

"I am the alpha of this pack, it is my job to know who the fuck comes into *my* territory, tries to touch *my* things, causes *my* pack problems, and I most certainly *can* keep you locked in a tower if I know it's where you're safest."

Alaric stared through the windshield, and Cleo had to admit his profile was just as attractive, if not more, when he was clenching his jaw.

"You don't own me, Alaric. You might be my alpha, but you are not my mate," she bit out.

Alaric gripped the steering wheel.

"You haven't asked about your *mate*." He scoffed. "I would have thought you'd be climbing the walls, trying to find your way back to him." His lips pulled back in a snarl, and it dawned on Cleo that he was jealous.

Of course, he doesn't know Mal is my mate.

He thinks it's Rocky.

Because we made it look like it was.

"Is Rocky okay?" she asked quietly.

Alaric let out a breath as they turned down the long driveway to the Thorne Estate. "Rocky is a fucking idiot, that's what he is. He knows better than to disobey, to..." Alaric paused, trying to regain himself. "He knows what we're up against and yet, he went against pack orders. Why? I don't know, but it doesn't change the fact he's injured. Car hit him, but the vamps got him first. They..." Alaric's voice caught in his throat and suddenly Cleo's heart raced faster, anxiety swelling in her stomach.

"How did you know where we were?" she asked warily.

Alaric huffed at her. "Even if you weren't mine, I'd still smell you a mile away. Your heat is like a fucking beacon."

"Is that why you came running? Because of my heat?" she nipped at him.

"I came running because you are *mine*, and I sensed you were in danger. Sawyer was supposed to take you home after your shift—"

"But he got carried away, because of my stupid heat, right?" Cleo could feel the warmth flushing into her cheeks as the memory of Sawyer mounting her pushed forth, along with the strange feelings and thoughts that came with it.

ARIEL DAWN

If those vamps hadn't shown up, would she have gone through with it?

The thought made her more than uncomfortable, and her thoughts wandered to Rocky and their shared kiss. While she wasn't certain if she felt anything deeper than friendship for the youngest Thorne, she felt a sting of guilt at the thought of his name. He'd taken a huge risk, sneaking her out of the estate, and then an even bigger one lying to his brother about the truth, about her heat.

"Is he going to be all right? Rocky? They didn't..." Cleo couldn't bear to finish the question, worried she'd have more than just lies to keep from Alaric, but also blood on her hands.

"They fucked him up. He lost a lot of blood, but Sawyer and I managed to fight them off, and they left. For now.

BLOOD OF MY ENEMY

But they'll be back. They want you."

The momentary relief she'd felt knowing Rocky was alive and not vampire fodder was soon eroded when Alaric's words hit her.

They want you.

Alaric tightened his grip on the steering wheel, the creaking sound echoing in the car as he drove around the front of the house. Against the light of the moon, the large mansion looked more like a haunted house than a home.

He put the car in park, turning it off, but neither of them opened their doors.

"Why would they want me?" she asked, dumbfounded.

Alaric turned to her. His hazel eyes had gone back to normal. "Because there are things you don't know about our kind. About *your* kind. Things that weren't disclosed for your own safety."

"My kind? What do you mean? I'm a wolf, just like you..." she said, confused.

Alaric's hand slid down the steering wheel, dropping into his lap. He looked at Cleo with an impenetrable gaze, his voice stern and commanding as ever. "There was a time when vampires and wolves left one another alone. Didn't meddle in each other's affairs, but... then, their population started dwindling."

"I don't see how any of that has to do with werewolves, or me for that matter," she said quietly.

Alaric let out a sigh, never taking his gaze off her. She could see the rise and fall of his chest, hear the steady rhythm of his heartbeat in the air, smell his earthy scent of musk and juniper leaves, and her insides felt warm. Not hot and all encompassing like when she was with Malcolm, but warm and cozy. Like a steady, slow-burning fire, and her wolf was most intrigued.

"Omegas are highly fertile. It's how you were designed, it's in your blood, and unfortunately, the Boracelli's latest queen has an appetite for supernatural blood. Says it gives her *special abilities*. Or at least, that's the rumor that's trickled through the channels. She needs an heir for her coven. Guess her consort studs are coming up short, and she's running out of options."

A strange sort of understanding dawned on Cleo in that moment, and the words fell out of her mouth instantly. "I'm not the first one they've tried to take, am I?" Her voice was barely a

ARIEL DAWN

whisper.

"No. You're not. That's why we wanted to keep you safe, in these walls." He motioned to the large, looming estate, and Cleo felt a pang of guilt.

Moonlight poured in through the windows, casting shadows on his fine features.

"This territory has been wolf territory for nearly a hundred years. No vampires dared come near it before, but now... now, the Boracellis have been spreading their black bat wings as far as the eye can see, and they'll take out whatever or whoever is in their way without a care to get what their queen demands."

The guilt, the pain that overcame Cleo at his words was heavy. She'd felt like a prisoner, waiting for a heat she thought would never come within those walls, never considering there was a reason beyond her own comprehension that they were keeping her locked up.

For her own protection.

Why didn't they tell her the truth?

Why hadn't the Oracle said anything, or for that matter, those she grew up with?

Her parents, or other pack members?

"And the others?" she asked, her voice shaking.

"They weren't in heat yet when they were taken. We'd found their bodies, drained like fucking juice boxes, but it wasn't enough for those goddamned devils." Alaric stared through the windshield, almost as if he was seeing something else.

No, remembering *someone* else. The glimmer of tears in the corner of his eyes

ARIEL DAWN

made Cleo's heart ache.

Who did you lose, Alaric?

"That's why we moved you here when we did. We knew they were going to attack your home."

Cleo's heart felt as if it was going to stop completely.

He knew?

Knew the vampires were coming and that's why she was moved so abruptly, en route when—

"Oh my God, Alaric—"

"Why did you do it?" he asked softly.

"Do what?" Cleo leaned closer, reaching out and setting her hand on his. She understood loss, too. After all, she'd lost many people, and the Thornes were all she knew, now.

And Malcolm Crowley.

She wanted to hate Alaric, but how

BLOOD OF MY ENEMY

could she?

He'd saved her life. She'd felt such guilt for not being there when the vampires attacked, when they'd killed her parents, but if he hadn't made the call when he did... She didn't dare to think what the vampires would have done with her, so she pushed the intrusive thoughts down.

"Why did you leave with him?" Alaric gazed down to where their hands touched and did not move.

His question felt heavy, as if he were asking more than why she decided to sneak out with Rocky. Almost as if he was asking why she hadn't chosen *him*.

The feel of his skin against her palm was just as warm, but it wasn't soft like Malcolm's. It was rough, and she could feel the fresh cuts from battle against

ARIEL DAWN

the pads of her fingertips.

"Because I wanted to be free," she answered. It was the truth, but somehow the words meant more. She wanted her life back. The days were long and arduous, even though they were comfortable. Everywhere she walked in the estate, she was under watch, even if everyone was accommodating to her needs. It was stifling, and after growing up on the edge of the mountains, free to roam as she wished, she hated it. She longed to run, to be *free*, to regain some semblance of normalcy.

To be more than the impending heat that everyone was waiting for.

Alaric turned to her, and she couldn't deny the cyclone within her that started to swirl once more. His gaze was not angry, or feral, as it had been earlier in the bar. Instead, it was full of sadness, of despair, and in the depths of her soul, she knew Alaric was a prisoner, too.

A prisoner of duty, born to uphold the order of his pack.

All the anger, all the control he displayed nothing but a mask to hide the broken, shattered man inside the beastly armor.

"Cleo, all you had to do was ask me. I—"

"Be honest, Alaric. Would you have granted me the freedom to do as I wanted? Or would you have put a leash on me, only allowing me as far as *you* wanted me to go?" she asked shakily.

Alaric leaned closer to her, resting his hand on top of hers, his thumb stroking the back of her knuckles. The feeling sent a shiver down her spine, and the heat returned. Cleo closed her eyes, trying to fight it.

"I would have given you anything you asked. You are my *omega*. For you, I would retrieve the moon, if you wanted it. I know the circumstances of you being here aren't the best, but I am not such an unreasonable man, Cleo. I need you to know that."

Cleo pursed her lips, trying to still her breath. Her wolf was pacing anxiously as she tried to regain control of her body, of her mind. Because Alaric's touch, his voice, his words—it was all too much. She wanted to believe him, but she couldn't. Not when their interactions over the past three weeks were scarce. They'd practically avoided each other since she arrived.

She also had a mate, so she knew the

feeling, knew deep within her being the unmistakable, magnetic pull one felt toward their mate, and it pained her to admit that she felt the fire for Alaric, too.

For Alaric Thorne, and she wanted so badly for it to be untrue, but the heat never lied.

It rarely stirred for multiple mates, though it had happened before.

Once.

Cleo opened her eyes to find Alaric's hazel ones staring back at her, tiny flecks of gold swimming in his irises. Somehow, they'd come closer, practically inches away from one another, like magnets drawn together.

"Do you feel that?" he breathed out.

Cleo held back the tears that begged to be set free. "Feel what?" she whispered in the silent darkness of

ARIEL DAWN

Alaric's Jeep.

"Our mate bond."

Cleo shivered at the words, not wanting to hear them any more than she wanted to acknowledge how true they were.

Because she did feel it.

She felt it deep within her as her wolf salivated, hungry for what it knew she was made for.

Hungry for *him.*

"Alaric, I can't." She let out a strangled sigh, a sob escaping.

"Cleo..." Her name on his tongue was like velvet, and she hated that it soothed her.

She pushed away from him, opening the door.

"Cleo..." he called as she walked with haste toward the doors of the estate, never looking back. And when Alaric's footsteps did not follow, she was relieved.

For in the silence, in the darkness of the halls of Thorne Estate, for the first time that night, Cleo felt like she could finally think.

Away from Alaric, from Malcolm, from the vampires.

And when she turned the corner to the hallway where her room was, she walked in and locked the door. Only then did she feel free.

14

"TELL ME EVERYTHING you know about werewolves," Malcolm said as he leaned against Hunter's motorcycle in the parking lot of Sally's Diner.

"I thought you didn't believe in werewolves, because there's no evidence," Hunter said with a raised eyebrow.

Mal shrugged. "Maybe I'm open to hear your theories."

BLOOD OF MY ENEMY

"Jesus, are you still drunk from last night or something? Why the change of heart?"

Mal's gaze followed the few people walking through the parking lot: a young couple, a single man, and a group of women. He wondered if all of them were like him or... like *her*. There'd been no marks, nothing other than that invisible tether for him to identify Cleo as anything other than human.

So, how could one tell if one was a werewolf?

"D and I hit a wolf last night. But, this wasn't any ordinary wolf at all. This thing was *huge*," he said pointedly. "I've seen a lot of animals in my time hunting with my dad, on the road with you guys, and this... this wasn't your run-of-the-mill wolf, Hunter. It had to be a werewolf

ARIEL DAWN

if I've ever seen one."

Hunter threw his leg over the seat, grabbing his helmet, but not putting it on immediately.

"Can you give me like an hour? I can get a comprehensive file together for you," he said the words so perfectly it was like he could have been a professor. A regular Indiana Jones. Or more accurately, an Indiana Jones in some sleek aviator shades twenty-four-seven.

"I think I can do that. I have some... research of my own to conduct, anyway," he said nonchalantly.

Hunter nodded, and the sound of Ava's laugh carried over.

Mal turned his head to see Ava and Vinny sitting on the wrought iron bench, both laughing at Dallas, who looked rather perturbed.

BLOOD OF MY ENEMY

"Sounds good, see you then," Hunter said as he threw on his helmet. He gunned the engine, then sped off, leaving Mal in the dust.

***

It was nearing noon, and the sun was downright brutal.

I'd forgotten how hot it gets up in these parts.

Ava walked ahead of him, through the woods, almost as if she knew exactly where they were going, exactly what they were looking for, but last Malcolm had checked, Ava didn't have werewolf radar.

Just vampire radar, which he had to admit was fairly handy.

"Daywalkers are fairly unlikely, especially up this way," Dallas said as he trudged through the forest next to him.

ARIEL DAWN

Mal turned, noting the sweat that had formed on Dallas's temples. "I don't think we're dealing with your average vampires. I don't think they're the ones we were tracking."

"What makes you say that?" Dallas asked, his voice even, despite the heat and their walking.

"Just call it a hunch," Mal answered.

"Ah, yes. The infamous Crowley Hunch," Dallas said with a smile.

"I don't want to say anything until I know for sure. Hunter's gathering some information for me, but I think we may have more than just vampires in these mountains. I think there's werewolves in these hills, too."

"Werewolves, huh?" Dallas said plainly, his eyes focused straight ahead on Ava, who was now a good distance ahead of them, moving fast, as always.

"Ava, slow down!" Mal hollered, trying to catch his breath, but she did not listen and kept going. Mal grumbled, silently cursing his sister. "Yup. That wolf we hit... There was no way that thing wasn't something supernatural."

"But no one's seen a werewolf. At least no one I know, and I know plenty of hunters."

"Just because you ain't seen it, doesn't mean it doesn't exist," Mal bit back.

Dallas smirked. "Touché. Now you sound like Hunter."

"The guy thinks outside the box, gotta appreciate that about him. Plus, he's a damn good bass player. He did say there was something off about the reports. Even Jones said he got a fishy

ARIEL DAWN

feeling."

"So what's your plan? Read up on Little Red Riding Hood, and then go hunting for grandma's cabin? Even if the werewolves are real, and they are here, what does that have to do with the vamps? They don't just vanish into thin air, contrary to belief. Which means if there are werewolves here *and* vamps—"

Ava stopped suddenly, looking back and forth between her surroundings, drawing both their attention.

"You feel something, Simba?" Mal called ahead.

Dallas stopped next to him, his muscles tensing as well.

The air smelled different here.

Almost like smoke.

Like fire.

"I did, but now... now, it's gone," she

answered.

Malcolm had the strangest feeling that they were being watched.

"What did you feel?" Dallas asked as he stopped next to her.

"Definitely a vampire. My wrist got all hot and tingly, but it was like it just... disappeared."

The sound of rustling brush caused Mal to draw his weapon, his stake, quickly. When a small rabbit hopped out from the bush behind him, he let out a deep sigh, feeling rather embarrassed.

"Fucking bunny," he huffed.

"We should get back," Dallas said. "There's nothing out here, man. Let's check back with Hunter and gather the others. After all, we should probably get our set list lined up for the show tonight," Dallas said as he turned to

ARIEL DAWN

head in the direction they'd come from.

"You're performing? Tonight?" Ava raised an eyebrow.

"Yeah, Dallas's idea."

"When the vampires will be out? Shouldn't we be—"

"Howlers is the watering hole and it's Saturday night. Any vamp worth their fucking blood will be at that bar tonight cruising for victims," Dallas answered definitively.

"Ah, so the plan is you guys get to jam out and I get to be vamp bait."

Mal didn't like the sound of such things, but he had to admit it was a solid plan.

"Jones will be there, too. So you won't be in any real danger," he assured her.

Ava scoffed. "I have killed my own share of vamps, Mal. Pretty sure I'm not the one in danger here," she said as she followed Dallas, tossing her hair over her shoulder in that quintessential conversation-is-over gesture she'd learned from cavorting with cheerleaders during her high school years.

Mal sighed as he followed his sister and partner out of the woods, praying whatever creature or whatever force was watching him kept its distance.

15

"EVIDENCE ISN'T MUCH to go off of since the wolves tend to lay low. A lot lower than vampires," Hunter said as he clicked through his PowerPoint.

Sometimes, Mal wondered where they'd all be if the life hadn't pulled them into the shadows, speculating that perhaps Hunter would have had some corporate desk job or some kind of gig where he got to make presentations and research history all day. He certainly looked the part with his black, square glasses and rolled up sleeves.

"What *do* you have for us, then?" Dallas asked, shifting his weight.

Ava peered over Hunter's shoulder at the bright computer screen.

"There is an abundance of lore about wolves that, if you aren't skilled, might just be misleading. But fortunately, for all of us, there's plenty of accounts of werewolves when you look at *vampire* history and lore. And we know there's plenty of evidence to support vampires..."

"So you compare the stories from what we do know with the lore. Smart thinking, Hunter," Ava said with an appreciative shrug.

Hunter smiled. "Thanks."

ARIEL DAWN

"In correlation to the vamps, what did you find?" Mal asked curiously.

Tito leaned back against the wall, twirling his knife, while Vinny took a seat on the other side of Hunter with a fresh cup of motel coffee in his grip.

"Well, for starters, vampires and werewolves don't like each other. In fact, there's plenty of history to support that both species have been at war for a long time with one another. Territorial disputes started to pop up around the mid to late 1800s among the covens with the whole expanse of America and the impending gold rush, and with the increase in the fur trade, it would appear that the vamps weren't the only enemy for the werewolves... and that is probably why we don't hear much about them."

BLOOD OF MY ENEMY

"Of course. Hunters," Vinny said, nodding in response.

Hunter snapped his fingers, pointing at Vinny. "Bingo."

"If I wanted a history lesson, Hunt, I'd go to school. While I can appreciate your scholarly dive into the first frontier, that doesn't tell me anything about werewolves and how to identify them, what their weaknesses are... if they are a danger to us—"

"Of course they're a danger. If we are to believe that they are here in Mahoning, then they are absolutely a threat to us," Dallas said definitively, raising a brow at Mal as if he'd completely lost his marbles to ask such a question.

"But they are natural born enemies of the bloodsuckers, right?" Mal asked, starting to feel hot and sweaty. As if he were under a microscope.

"The enemy of our enemy is our friend, right?" Mal asked nervously.

Tito looked at him as he stopped twirling his knife, his bright, blue eyes cold. "The enemy of my enemy is not my ally. That is not how it works, Mal. You, of all people, know this."

Ava looked back and forth between them all. "What's he talking about Mal?" she asked curiously.

Mal shrugged, not wanting to think about the losses he'd endured in the early days of hunting. How he'd been naive and trusting of those he assumed had his best interest because they were fighting for the same thing, for the same cause. He thanked his lucky stars he'd had Dallas to back him up. Even then,

BLOOD OF MY ENEMY

Dallas seemed to have a knack for reading between the lines and had saved his ass on more than one occasion, and ever since, Malcolm had become wiser. Though trust and allies were hard to come by, he looked around the room at the collection of misfits he'd found along the way. His gaze settled on his sister, a conflicted sting settled in his heart at knowing she, too, had been tarnished by those she trusted.

"All I'm saying, is if we're after the same target, maybe they aren't so bad."

"Maybe. But Mama always said not to trust anything with teeth," Ava said.

"Humans have teeth…" Vinny said, cocking his head to the side.

Ava rolled her eyes. "Yeah, and humans can't be trusted to do shit. History is pretty *evident* with that," she

ARIEL DAWN

bit back.

Vinny frowned. "Yeah, I guess you have a point there."

"So how do we pick these suckers out of a crowd?" Dallas asked as he sat on the bed next to Ava, causing all of them on the bed to shift as the mattress dipped to support his larger frame.

"Well, according to the lore, at the base of everything, a werewolf is just a shapeshifter. Technically, lore calls them the original shapeshifters, being on this earth longer than we probably have recorded history for, and like any other shapeshifter, they tend to all have a similar look that is conducive to their climate. Like the animals they shift into, they have a penchant for forests, and most seem to gravitate, if the stories are any indication, to moderate climates and stick to mountains, forests, and civilizations that are low in population. The alpha werewolves, the ones that govern their pack, tend to be bigger in size both in wolf form and in human form. A pack will usually all have a similar look, similar build. Betas are still big, not as big as alphas, but definitely not your average build. Omegas, the females tend to be on the smaller side."

"Yeah, but that's still not very reliable," Ava said as she shifted her weight to accommodate Dallas next to her, but with the way the mattress dipped it did not seem to help and she fell against his side with an annoyed huff. "I mean, if we were to suspect every gym bro was a werewolf, we'd have to throw Dallas in that category and we know he's not a werewolf," she said with

ARIEL DAWN

a chuckle as she turned to him over her shoulder, flashing him a mischievous glare. "Or is there something you're not telling the rest of us?" she teased.

Dallas shoved her with annoyance as his jaw clenched. "You know I ain't no fucking shapeshifter, Ava."

"Nope, just a grumbly, old man," she said with a giggle, and Mal couldn't help but let out a laugh, the others letting out small laughs of their own.

"True," Hunter said when they'd all stopped laughing. "There is one thing, though, that seems to be a pattern, or at least pops up more than once in the research." He cleared his throat.

"What?" Mal said, leaning closer and looking at the PowerPoint.

"Scent," Hunter said plainly. "Shapeshifters are extremely sensitive to smells and sounds, like the animals they shift into, and in all the stories, the appearance of a werewolf always accompanies the notation of the smell of fire. Like burning wood."

"And we've got big dudes who smell like a campfire. Anything else?" Ava said as she leaned back further into Dallas's space, causing him to shift once again, to make room for her. He grumbled, cursing under his breath but moved anyway, and Mal had to stifle another laugh.

"It's inconclusive, but the vampire histories say that their eyes have a golden glow or something before they shift, but it's only mentioned one or two times in reference to the territory wars in the 1920s, upstate New York. When the covens were really starting to enforce their boundaries, especially this one coven that seems to come up a lot. The Boracellis, I think it was."

Malcolm perked up. He'd heard the name before. In fact, he'd held the name for quite a long time.

In the early days of the investigation of his parents' deaths, he hadn't had much luck finding the vampires responsible. Untrained, he hadn't known how to track them, and his research was relegated to asking hunters, among others, what they saw, what they knew.

That was how he met Dallas.

He'd asked him his knowledge of any visiting covens, any supernatural happenings in Salem at the time, and Dallas had turned up the knowledge he sought.

The coven who was in town, picking

off slayers and hunters like his parents, were not just any coven of vampires, but as Dallas told him, a *high* coven. A collection of powerful vamps that had been around for centuries that seemed untouchable.

The Boracellis.

Malcolm had been chasing leads, trying to find the Boracellis ever since, convinced that perhaps, they had something to do with his parents' murders, or at the very least, knew who did it. He'd often fantasized about finding them, their queen, Francesca. Torturing the answers out of them before finally staking them and burning them to the ground.

"So, big dudes who smell like a campfire and have golden eyes, okay then," Ava drawled sarcastically.

ARIEL DAWN

"Yes, that means be on the lookout tonight when you're patrolling the bar." Tito nodded at her.

"How do you kill a werewolf?" Ava asked.

Hunter closed down his laptop as he got up from the center of the bed. "Again, it's inconclusive, but the vampire stories suggest that their venom is toxic to werewolves, so that's one way to kill them, but for us, the best bet would be silver. Most of the stories are from a long time ago, and supernatural weaponry wasn't like it is now. It was basically wooden stakes, holy water, and silver. Your monster hunting trinity. If it didn't die with one of those three things, you were fucked."

Ava nodded. "Shoot anything with a silver bullet and it's likely to go down like a sack of potatoes, so I guess that makes sense."

"Silver knife works, too," Tito said with a grin as he pressed the tip of his blade against the pad of his finger, drawing a small drop of blood before letting up, sliding it in his mouth, and licking it clean.

The notion was creepy at best, but the lot of them knew, where Tito was concerned, it was best to just let him go. The man was loyal as a dog, but they all knew he was missing a screw somewhere. It was always helpful to have a madman on your team who was loyal to you and your cause.

"Oh darn. Left my Gucci blades at home," she nipped, her voice drenched in sarcasm.

"You can use mine. After all, I'll be

occupied on stage, anyway..." Vinny said as he shifted closer to Ava, handing her his small, silver dagger.

Malcolm watched as she grabbed it from him, her eyes lighting up with excitement at the idea of killing a werewolf.

His blood went cold.

"Thanks, Vin," she said with a smile, and he nodded in response.

"Thanks, Hunter. We've got a few hours until sound check, so now would be the time, if everyone needs, to catch some rest or get something to eat or whatever," Mal said as he turned away from the group and headed for the door.

"Sounds good. I'll call Jones and give him the details. Have him meet us at Howlers before the show starts at eight," Vinny said.

BLOOD OF MY ENEMY

They all nodded in agreement, scattering like ants as they left.

16

"IT WAS AN accident. I'd taken Cleo out, thinking maybe a little fresh air would help. Rocky and Sawyer came as well, and we just happened to run into the vamps."

Cleo pressed herself against the wall, listening closely. She was surprised to hear the lies tumble off Alaric's tongue so smoothly, especially to his parents, Armand and Kitania Thorne.

BLOOD OF MY ENEMY

Growing up on the other side of the ridge, she hadn't known many of the surrounding packs. Though, the Thorne name was one that *everyone* knew, even if they only knew it by name. They were a strong pack, and most of the reason the rest of them could live in peace.

Kitania and Armand were ruthless in upholding pack law, in keeping the area free from threats. They were also adamant in keeping the secrecy of werewolf life, sticklers for laying low, considering they lived among humans.

The notion that Alaric was lying to them did not go unnoticed with the weight of his action.

Rocky had covered with her, for her, so she would not have to tell Alaric the truth about her mate bond.

Now Alaric was lying for her and for

ARIEL DAWN

Rocky.

How many more lies must we tell?

"You know Clementine is safer here, Alaric," Armand said sternly.

"I know she is, but is she not safe with me? Wherever I am? I am the alpha of this pack now, for Christ's sake. If she isn't safe with me, who will she be safe with?" he bit back.

Armand let out a growl of his own in response.

Alaric's words settled with her, causing her stomach to twist again, and she fought to ignore it. A hand at her back startled her and she jumped, almost letting out a sound.

"Boo," Sawyer said with a mischievous smile.

"You scared the shit out of me, Sawyer."

BLOOD OF MY ENEMY

"Anyone tell you, you look cute when you're scared," he teased her, and she frowned. "Spying on big brother, I see." Sawyer twisted his lips, all teasing now aside.

"I-I didn't mean for any of this to happen, and I don't want any trouble for Alaric..." she said, averting her eyes.

"Alaric is a lot of things, one of them a damn good fixer. If anyone can smooth all of this over, it's him," he said as he gently pressed his fingers against her back, an invitation to walk with him.

She obliged, yet the concern was still prevalent as she walked farther away from her hidden post. "I shouldn't have left, should've told Rocky no, I should've—"

"Shhh. Don't do that. Shoulda, woulda, coulda. It was fate. It was bound to happen." Sawyer ran his fingertips up and down the small space where his hand lay, and Cleo had to admit it was a rather soothing feeling. For the moment, it helped still her nerves.

They walked down the long corridor, exiting through one of the side doors and into the courtyard.

"You really believe that? Aren't you angry your brother is injured? Because of me?" Cleo could feel the tears starting to well in her eyes at the words. She hadn't mustered up the courage to see Rocky yet, though she'd been thinking about it all morning.

"My brother stirred your heat. He did what Alaric and I wished we could have done." Sawyer stopped, turning to Cleo. Against the landscape of carefully cultivated roses and rhododendrons, against the large stone fountain, he looked just like some picturesque romance novel cover hero. Like his brothers, he had the same dark hair, the same sun-kissed skin, but where Alaric had the chiseled jaw with a perpetual five o'clock shadow and Rocky was smooth and clean-shaven, Sawyer was somewhere in between. Scruffy, yet sophisticated, almost like...

Malcolm.

The name dredged up his image in Cleo's mind instantly. Malcolm was the average human build, not muscular and defined like any of the Thorne brothers, with long, dark hair that begged to have Cleo's fingers twisted in it, with bright, amber eyes that could make her blood heat on sight.

For a human, her mate held quite a

power. Just the thought of tangling her fingers in his hair, of feeling the scratchiness of his facial hair against her neck again, caused an unexpected wetness to blossom between her thighs, and caused her insides to ache.

This is so frustrating!

How does anyone make it through this goddamned heat?

Sawyer must have noticed her sudden change, and the reality of that caused her to blush furiously as he smiled wickedly at her.

"You feeling okay there, Cleo?" He let his tongue dart out, licking his lips and she crossed her arms, refusing to look at him.

"I'm fine, thanks."

"All you have to do is ask. Just because Rocky stirred your heat doesn't mean he has to be the one to—"

"I said I'm fine," Cleo said, her voice much sharper.

Sawyer put his hands in the air, in a truce. "I wasn't trying to piss you off. Just letting you know if you need to let off some steam, I'm here. I'm not going to pretend to know what you're going through, but I'd regret it if I didn't shoot my shot, you know?" he said with a sigh.

"Shoot your shot, huh? How would Alaric feel about that?" Cleo said, feeling bolder for the moment, agitated. She narrowed her eyes at Sawyer.

"I'm the beta of this pack, it wouldn't be unheard of if you picked me. There's been plenty of betas who have mated with their alpha's omega." Sawyer shrugged.

"Quite confident, aren't you?"

ARIEL DAWN

Sawyer leaned against the fountain, raising an eyebrow at her. "I know what I have to offer," Sawyer said as he dragged his thumb over his lips.

Cleo rolled her eyes. "Maybe I don't want what you're offering." She turned away from Sawyer, heading farther into the courtyard and into the garden.

"What do you want then, baby? Say the word and I'll make it happen," Sawyer said as he came up behind her, closing in on her.

Cleo spun around, her wolf rising to the surface. "I want to come and go as I please! I want to have space to breathe, which I can't do when I'm locked up in this fucking house all day when I have the lot of you breathing down my neck because you're all angling to fuck me!" she exploded.

BLOOD OF MY ENEMY

Sawyer advanced into her space, his lips pulling back enough to show his fangs, his eyes shimmering with golden flecks.

Cleo stumbled on the stone pavement, her hands bracing against the stone terrace.

Sawyer angled his head, his eyes predatory. "We were made to fuck you, Cleo. Not our fault you smell like goddamned milk and honey and look like a wet dream. It's not our fault the animals inside of us take over when you're in the room," he growled out. "It's instinct, it's nature."

"Well, you can tell your animal and nature to back off. I'm more than just a breeding machine for all your future pups you know!" She could feel the anger in her rising, unsure of where it was coming from, but not being able to stop it.

"You know I never would have pegged you for a brat, but I can't say I dislike it," Sawyer said as he stepped closer, backing Cleo up against the wall.

She felt hot from her head to her toes, her mind swimming. "Back off, Sawyer," she said with a growl as he reached a hand out, running his fingers along her jaw. The touch made her shiver.

"You can't honestly tell me you don't want this. Every part of my being *knows* you do. I can smell your arousal, and even if I couldn't, I can see it in your eyes, the way you press your thighs together, and I saw the look in your eyes last night in the woods. You want me."

Cleo looked up into his eyes, remembering their moment in the woods. How she had felt in that moment, she knew he was right. She wanted *release*. To give in to the heat, but it wasn't Sawyer she wanted.

Not then.

Not now.

She pushed him away with the palm of her hand. "You're wrong, Sawyer. I don't want you. I just want to be free of this damn heat." She left abruptly, picking up her pace as she left Sawyer alone in the courtyard.

I need to get out of this house.

I need—

Without looking where she was going, she ran into a brick wall. Well, he should have been a brick wall, if the solidness of his chest had anything to say about it.

"Cleo, is everything all right? You look upset..." Alaric steadied her with his

ARIEL DAWN

hands.

Her eyes widened in surprise. "Alaric, what are you doing here? I thought you were with your parents..."

Alaric smirked. "How would you know where I was? Were you spying on me?"

"What? No, I—"

"Just can't stay out of trouble, can you?" he said shaking his head.

"I just didn't want you to get in trouble for my mistake," she answered honestly.

Alaric ran his fingers along his jaw, feigning a look of deep thought. "I'm not in trouble. Neither are you. As far as everyone knows, it was my idea to take you to Howlers, my brothers were just along for the ride." He shrugged.

"And my heat?" she asked, curious to know if her lie was being upheld.

"I told them the truth. Rocky stirred your heat, but that you hadn't acted on it yet."

Yet.

"Yeah, Sawyer didn't seem to get that memo," she grumbled.

Alaric's eyes widened, a golden glow coming over them. "Sawyer? What did he do, did he—"

"No. He didn't do anything. Just got a little cocky is all. Acted like he was God's gift to omegas or something, but I told him to get lost."

Alaric's lips pursed in a tight line. "I'll take care of him."

At the realization of his words, Cleo worried she'd said too much. "You're not going to hurt him, are you?"

Alaric cocked his head to the side inquisitively. "Why, do you not want me to?" he asked, confused.

"I mean, Sawyer's a bit of an asshole, but it's not *his* fault his animal's going cuckoo for my cocoa puffs, right?" she said sarcastically.

Alaric took a step closer to her, but he kept his distance. His eyes still shone with the gold shifter glow, but he wasn't looming or lumbering. Instead, the verity of his tone implied how serious he was. "Our animals respond to your heat because it's what we were made for, but that doesn't mean you don't have a choice, Cleo. You always have a choice."

His words stirred her wolf, her insides becoming warm. She stepped closer to him, and even though she was much smaller, for the first time since she'd arrived at the Thorne Estate, she felt taller.

BLOOD OF MY ENEMY

"So, if I didn't choose any of you, what would happen?" Her words were barely a whisper.

Alaric stepped closer, reaching his hand out to push a stray strand of hair behind her ear, dropping his hand immediately afterward. "You were sent here to be *my* omega. Preferably to bear my children, but pack law isn't as picky as long as it is a Thorne heir. It would be unheard of, in your case, as the heat typically chooses its mate. It's instinct. I'm not an idiot, Cleo. I know Rocky stirred your heat, and before that, you had already had a deeper connection with him than with Sawyer and me, and the probability you will choose Rocky to mate with is high. There is no deadline. You can take as much time as you need to make your choice, and I will fully

ARIEL DAWN

support that, even if it means you don't choose me."

Alaric looked into her eyes, and she could see the reflection of herself in them, but she could also see sadness, pain, guilt. Such things made her heart ache, and in that moment, she wanted to bare her soul to Alaric Thorne, the way he was bearing his soul to her. But she knew that would only end in more pain and guilt, and she refused to add to Alaric's already alarming load.

"I won't bullshit you, Cleo. I want you. I have wanted you since the day you showed up on my doorstep, looking like everything I had ever dreamed of, and you weren't even in heat yet. I am not good at this sort of thing. The emotional thing. The connection thing. I don't know how to be what you want, but I will always be what you need, I can promise you that. I want you." He reached out, taking her hand in his in the softest of gestures, and it broke her heart to feel the kindness, the sweetness of such a touch.

"But I will not force you into something you don't want. I want you to choose me willingly. I won't pretend that I'll be okay if you choose Rocky because even if you do choose him, it won't change the fact that I'll want you then just as I do know, but..." His voice caught in his throat, and he let out a deep breath, and Cleo could feel the tears in her eyes.

"But if you do not choose any of us, I will stand behind your choice. Even if I don't agree with it." He ran his thumb over her knuckles and the cyclone started to swirl once more.

"Alaric," she whispered his name, but it meant so much more.

"I only have one thing to ask of you in return," he said with a soft smile.

Cleo wiped the wetness from the corner of her eyes. "Anything," she said as she forced a smile.

"Well, I did tell my parents it was my idea to bring you to Howlers, so I'd at least like the same opportunity you afforded my brother. I'd like..." He swallowed hard, and Cleo could see he was nervous. "I thought about what you said, about freedom. About wanting to get out of this foreboding house." He gestured around the large, elegant, yet haunting-looking decor.

"I thought maybe if you were up for it, we could check out Howlers tonight.

Just you and me. There's a band playing tonight and—"

"Yes," Cleo said instantly. The prospect of getting out of Thorne Estate, of having fun, was too much to turn down, and if she was being honest, it was the least she could do for Alaric considering the amount of lies he was unknowingly upholding for her.

"Yes?" he asked, his eyes widening in surprise.

Cleo nodded. "Yes, Alaric. It's a date."

17

MALCOLM WAS SURPRISED to see the crowd at Howlers, given the fact it wasn't even seven thirty. Apparently, Dallas's decision to book a gig was a good idea and word traveled fast.

Blood Of My Enemy wasn't famous by any stretch, but the band did have its fans, even if it was a small group. Though with a lackluster schedule of performing, and a lack of updates and social media, it was more than a surprise when they came across those who knew who they were.

The bar was hopping, and Mal wondered how long it would take to get a beer. He made his way through the crowded floor, figuring now would be as good a time as any.

Ava sat at the bar, talking to Jones, who was doing the poorest job of flirting Mal had ever seen. He couldn't help but roll his eyes. No matter where she went, it seemed like Ava had a string of moths that always followed.

"Gonna have to fight them off with a stick," his father had joked when Ava made the cheerleading squad.

"Or we'll just have to teach her how to use a really big stick, Pete," his mother purred.

ARIEL DAWN

Mal rolled his eyes as one of the girls on the bottom tossed Ava in the air.

"She's going to be a heartbreaker if she's anything like her mama," his father said as he pulled his wife close, planting a kiss on her cheek.

"Might need to put Malcolm on clean up duty," he said with a wink to Mal.

Mal slid between Jones and Ava, breaking up the duo's titillating conversation.

Ava crossed her legs, the holes in her black jeans eliciting a contrasting show of skin. She'd opted to tie what looked like one of Dallas's shirts around her waist, her Led Zeppelin shirt rolled up and tucked under to expose her midriff. Though he knew the reason for her showing an excess of skin was primarily for vampire catching, it still made him feel a sense of protectiveness, and he contemplated throwing his jacket over her.

"Ain't gonna catch any bats if you're staring at each other all night," he drawled instead.

Ava flicked her hair over her shoulder.

Jones actually had the audacity to blush and look flustered. "I wasn't—"

"Take your position. We go on in fifteen," Mal said, not even bothering to wait for Jones's response.

Jones scoffed, grabbing his beer and sauntering off toward the entrance of the bar, not saying a word, leaving Malcolm and Ava alone.

"You're such a killjoy, Mal, really. They're not even here, yet. I'd know. You need to settle down. Have some fun," she said as she took a sip of her whiskey.

"How'd you get that? You're not even old enough to drink." Mal furrowed his eyes at Ava who smirked.

"Jones doesn't know that."

Mal huffed in annoyance. "Try to stay sober for this assignment, please."

"That's the pot calling the kettle black," she drawled as she set her drink down, covering it with her hand.

Mal shot her a glare. "I'll have you know I'm just as lethal drunk as I am sober, if not better."

Ava rolled her eyes at him. "Whatever you have to tell yourself to make yourself feel better," she bit out.

"Speaking of vamps, where's your little bloodsucking tagalong?"

Ava's shoulders tensed immediately, her demeanor shifting from her carefree, adventurous spirit to something else. "Cas? How the hell should I know," she said with disdain. "I don't keep tabs on him."

Mal shrugged. "No, but he certainly keeps tabs on you. I mean, he has followed you across state lines before. Just curious if we were going to have another pain-in-the-ass vampire to worry about."

Ava shifted off her barstool. "I don't want to talk about Cassius. Can we please talk about *anything* but him?"

"What is it, Ava?" Mal tensed immediately upon her response, the worry flooding him that something happened. Something while he was gone, something that— "You didn't—"

"Oh my God! No! Why do you always think I'm going to end up screwing the vampire, Mal? Seriously?" she bit back. "Have a little more faith in me! It's never going to happen!"

"If you would let me finish! That's not what I was going to say!" Mal snapped, and Ava recoiled.

"Don't freaking yell at me! I'm not one of your misfits you can just boss around."

"All I'm saying is that vampire is getting way too comfortable with you."

"That *vampire* saved my life, Mal. But yes, I know he's comfortable. I need him comfortable, so I can put a fucking stake through his heart," she snapped.

"Just don't get too close you forget your end game, Ava. Thrall is a powerful thing."

"Yeah, I know. So are claiming marks, but you don't see me throwing myself at

BLOOD OF MY ENEMY

Cas, now do you?" Ava said as she grabbed her whiskey and drained the remainder. "Now if you're done lecturing me, you'll have to excuse me, I have some vampires to hunt."

***

Malcolm looked out at the crowd surrounding the stage as he played the opening riff to Ted Nugent's *Cat Scratch Fever*. The sound of his guitar above the hoots and hollers was music to his ears, giving him a high that he hadn't felt in far too long.

It was addicting, and he wanted more.

Needed it.

The energy of the crowd fed him in a way food and connection never could. Dallas commanded the stage as he always did, and the crowd loved him, as

ARIEL DAWN

they always did no matter where they went.

It felt good to be on stage, to be himself. It was strange that the place Malcolm Crowley felt the most free was on display in front of a room of total strangers.

From his vantage point, he could see everything. The door where Jones stood, the floor where the crowd had collected, the bar where Ava hung out while sipping on whiskey.

Just as they finished the last notes of *Cat Scratch Fever,* segueing into Motley Crue's *Wild Side,* Ava perked up as two men entered the bar. One was tall and pale with bright red hair. The other was of equal stature with dark brown, shoulder length hair. Their pale skin and well dressed ensembles made them stick out like sore thumbs.

Vampires.

Jones looked at him just as Ava descended from the bar, disappearing through the crowd.

Malcolm kept his eyes on her. They played through *Wild Side* into several other songs, and just as they were starting the last song before their intermission, Dio's *Rainbow in the Dark*, the scent of fire filled his airways.

The magnetic pull was stronger than before, and he knew exactly where to look. His eyes locked onto familiar, green-blue pools, and his throat went dry.

But Cleo was not alone.

She was with the tall, hulking man who'd practically knocked his door down.

ARIEL DAWN

Her boyfriend.

Mal didn't wish to tear his eyes away, but he needed to keep his sight on Ava and the vampires who were among the crowds. And as he found his sister, his heart sunk. For there, in the middle of the crowd, stood Ava and the two vampires, dancing together, much too closely for his liking.

Ava turned her head, looking directly at him, then at Dallas, the slight nod of her head telling them exactly where she was going.

Out back.

To slay.

The crowd cheered as the band finished their set, and the hunters dispersed quickly from the stage while Ava and the vamps disappeared.

18

THE THICK CROWD made it hard to move, as everyone was well lubricated with drink at this point, and the music blaring over the speakers mingled with the jukebox tunes making it difficult to hear amidst all the shouts and talking.

Just as Malcolm made it through the crowd to the exit, he ran into the body of a solid statue.

"Where do you think you're going?"

he asked, his voice deep and commanding.

"None of your fucking business, asshole," Mal bit out, trying to get around the lumbering man.

"If you came back for Cleo, you're wasting your time," the man said.

Malcolm looked up into the eyes of the tall man who was pissing him off right now. He needed to get out back to Ava, to his squad, but something about the candor of this man's voice held him in place, and then he saw his eyes.

Flecks of gold glittered in the man's dark brown eyes, and he smelled like... *fire.*

Werewolf.

"I'm not here for your fucking girlfriend. I'm here for bigger things," he said as he tried to advance, but the man stopped him, blocking his path. The angry look he gave Mal made his hair on his neck stand.

"I don't believe you," he snarled.

Mal could feel himself becoming more agitated and so he pushed against the man. "Let me pass. My sister is out there, and she's in trouble."

The man narrowed his eyes at Mal, almost as if he was trying to decide if he was telling the truth or not.

What is this asshole's problem?

Just then, a shrill shriek carried through the air, and Mal's blood chilled. A pain struck deep within him and he knew.

He knew his mate was in danger, and so he didn't think twice about shoving her boyfriend out of the way, adrenaline coursing through him.

BLOOD OF MY ENEMY

He ran out the exit, with the werewolf right behind him. When they'd made it outside, it was clear to see there were more vamps than they'd anticipated. What they thought had been three or four, a small collection, was in reality about seven or eight, and it was a damn brawl.

Dallas laid his stake into one of the vampires as Tito held him by the arms, Vinny throwing punches at one while Hunter was pressed into the asphalt, a woman vampire with long, red hair snapping at him with her fangs, and then he saw her.

Cleo.

She was kicking, fighting against a vampire with jet-black, oily, slicked-back hair.

Ava lunged for the vampire who had

ARIEL DAWN

Hunter, scrambling as fast she could.

A ferocious growl echoed in the air, and Malcolm could feel the hairs standing all over his body at the deep, animal sound. He didn't have time to think, only act as he sped off directly for the vampire who was carrying Cleo toward a black sedan. He barely noticed the large wolf beside him, running toward her as well.

"Don't fucking touch her, you son of a bitch!" Mal hollered, driven by an instinct, a need he'd never felt before. It was like magnetism, like a force had completely hijacked him and his brain.

Nothing mattered except her.

Except knowing she was safe.

Mal swung at the vampire while the wolf snapped its jaws at his legs.

The vampire hissed as Cleo continued

to kick and fight against his hold, and then, the vampire let out a bloodcurdling scream of his own.

Cleo reared her head back, blood trickling down her face.

The werewolf pounced on the vampire just as Malcolm brought out his stake, aiming for its heart. Behind him, the sounds of wet crunching were apparent, and so were the growls.

More wolves, great.

The vampire reared its head back, angling for the wolf beside him and Malcolm shifted it away.

The strange instinct to protect this wolf he didn't know was jarring, but he didn't have time to question it.

Not now.

Cleo wriggled out of the vampire's hold, scrambling to her feet. She stood

ARIEL DAWN

tall, if a five-foot-three woman could be considered tall, and in the light of the moon, with the blood running down her chin, and the golden, unmistakable glow in her eyes, Mal knew there was no denying the truth.

Cleo Srirocco was a werewolf.

And beyond all that made sense, she was his mate, and nothing would change that.

Nothing could change what was fate.

The moment their eyes locked, he knew. The feral look in her eyes, the bloodlust he'd seen on far too many vampires' faces right before he'd killed them.

He could *feel* it.

Her *need*.

Cleo ran off for the woods, the large, black wolf running behind her, and Mal did not think twice about running after her.

"Mal!" Dallas called, but it was no use.

Mal ran into the woods as if he was under a spell, because, in a way, he was. The vampires descended behind him, and he turned over his shoulder to see Hunter coughing, trying to catch his breath, Ava beside him.

Vinny lit a vampire on fire, and Tito and Hunter were right behind him, running to catch the vamps and the wolf who was chasing Cleo, and he followed her, followed them into the darkness, determined to put a stake through their chests if it was the last thing he did.

19

THE TRANSITION TO wolf was much easier this time for Cleo. It came without warning, without hesitation, almost as if her animal knew in the presence of its natural born enemy what it must do.

Alaric caught up to her, nipping at her as he tried to communicate, though Cleo couldn't understand. There was only one instinct she had at this moment, and that was to run.

BLOOD OF MY ENEMY

To escape.

A whimper from behind her alerted her, and she turned to see one of the vampires had caught up to them, and wrapped its long, sinuous arms around Alaric, lifting him off the ground, which was no small feat.

"Leave him alone!" she hollered, but it only came out as a loud, barking, angry growl.

Because she was a wolf now.

The vampire held Alaric tight, his neck in their long, spindly fingers, poised to strike and break it. A strange swell of protectiveness flared within her, something so deep and so strong it was like an entity all its own. The need, no, the desire, to protect what was hers.

Her alpha.

Alaric.

ARIEL DAWN

Her mate.

She knew it just as she knew Malcolm was. And the desire, the need, to protect him as well was like a hurricane within her, propelling her toward them.

Cleo lunged forward, her jaws colliding with the vamp's leg.

The vampire let out a shrill shriek.

Behind her, she could hear the others advancing.

The vampire tried to shake her off, but she did not let go.

She jumped as a hand set against her fur, a voice she recognized coaxing her to let go.

"I'm going to light this son of a bitch up in flames, and then you're going to run with me. We need to get you out of here, somewhere safe. Do you understand?" Malcolm's voice was stern and stirred her wolf in a way she hadn't expected.

She whined, turning her head to Alaric, then back to Mal. Trying to make him understand. Cleo wanted to bite. To tear this enemy apart limb from limb, and the desire to do so was so very strong, warring with the instinct to do as her mate asked.

Alaric twisted and turned in the vampire's grasp, trying to escape, but it was no use.

What about Alaric, what about—

"I'll do my best, but you have to run!" he answered her as if he could hear her thoughts, as if he could actually understand her. It would have to be enough.

There was no time to think as

ARIEL DAWN

Malcolm plunged the stake into the vampire's chest. He struck a match and lit the vampire on fire, the flames licking his skin as the scent of death and decay filled the air, the flames reflecting in her eyes.

Alaric jumped, but it was clear he was hurt, he wasn't moving very well.

"Run! Cleo, Run!" Mal said as he shoved her, a vampire coming up from behind him.

She didn't wait this time.

She ran.

She ran, faster, farther until the trees became blurred lines, until her paws hit the asphalt, and then she ran some more until she came to the Moonflower Motel, and there she waited, praying Alaric or Malcolm would come to find her.

BLOOD OF MY ENEMY

She couldn't have been certain how long she waited, but when the candy apple red Chevelle pulled into the parking lot, once the headlights dimmed, she slowly crept up to the car, feeling more afraid than she had in a long time. When Malcolm opened the door, she wasn't sure what she expected to see, but a large, naked and bloody Alaric wasn't it.

There was no light other than the moonlight, the flickering ambiance of the Moonflower's Street signs, and the buzzing, fading light in front of Malcolm's room.

Malcolm didn't look so hot himself. He was dirty and bloody, and his shirt looked as if he'd been mauled. Fresh, red scratches peeked through the tears in his shirt.

ARIEL DAWN

She shifted without thinking, heading right for him.

For him and Alaric.

"Mal, is he, are you—"

Her hand slid over his chest, over the tears in his shirt. His skin was warm to the touch and still moist. She pulled her hand away, noting the blood on her fingertips.

"I'm okay, he's... okay, I think," Mal said, his breathing rapid.

"I'm so sorry. I didn't know they would be there, the vampires. I—"

Mal's lips crushed hers with a fury she'd never felt from anyone in all her life. His hands slid around her waist, pulling her against him as he ravaged her mouth with his.

Relief, pain, and guilt flooded her, the sounds of Alaric's breathing loud in her ears.

"You're okay," he breathed out, his hands sliding up her back. Cleo rested her hands on his throat, feeling his racing pulse.

She kissed him back, the heat within her a raging fire. "I'm okay," she whispered back.

Malcolm pulled away. "We killed them," he said as he leaned his forehead against hers.

She let her fingers stroke his silky hair, relishing in the touch. She barely knew Malcolm Crowley, yet, it was as if she had known him her entire life. It was as if, on some deeper level, she'd always known him. Like he was always a part of her, waiting to be awakened.

Instinct took over as her wolf rushed to the surface, and she took his bottom

ARIEL DAWN

lip in between her teeth, sucking, nibbling, tasting the blood on his lip that had not dried yet from his roundabout with the creatures of the night.

Malcolm hardened against her, a deep rumble sounding from his throat. "Cleo..." he groaned, but she did not relent.

Instead, her hands traveled down his shirt, resting on his belt, her fingers making fast work.

His hands settled underneath her thighs, gripping tightly as he ground himself against her palm.

"Malcolm." She breathed his name like a silent prayer.

"We shouldn't." His voice was strained, his words betraying his body.

Alaric groaned in the back seat.

"Are you rejecting me?" she breathed

out, her hands shaking as they hovered over Mal's erection.

Mal looked into her eyes.

"No. I'm not rejecting *you*. But..." He closed his eyes, pursing his lips. "Your boyfriend is half alive in the back seat of my car, and I'm not exactly the voyeuristic type or the public sex type." He let out a small, nervous laugh. "We need to get you and Van Helsing back where you belong." His voice darkened, and Cleo could hear the sadness in it.

"I belong with you. You are my mate, and he's not my boyfriend," she said as her gaze settled on Malcolm.

"I don't know any more about this fucking bond shit than you do, but I know that's a lie. Because I can *feel* it, and even if I couldn't, I'd know. I can smell a lie a mile away." He leaned his forehead against hers once more, licking his lips as he closed his eyes.

In that moment, she knew.

Her heart had already started to break.

Malcolm Crowley was rejecting her.

Rejecting their bond.

"You are leaving." She let the words fall out of her mouth, tears coming to her eyes. The heat pulsed within her as she pressed herself against him, needing to feel him more than ever at the thought of losing him.

"I have to leave. I'm not, thi-this can't happen between us. I—" He let out a deep breath. "I left my party to chase after you. They could have died, too. My sister, my friends. I can't let that happen, Cleo. I can't put them in danger like that again, and I can't put you in danger, either."

"You don't get to make that call, Malcolm..."

"Yes, I do. Because I know what happens to the people I love. They die." He pushed her away and she hated how it felt. He removed his shirt, handing it to her. "Here." He held it out to her, and she grabbed it, their hands touching for just a moment.

She pulled the shirt on, her gaze settling on his sleek, pale chest, the scars across it making her heart ache, making her stomach swirl. Beaten, dirty, bloody Mal had to be one of the most attractive things she'd ever laid eyes on, and the blood, the claw marks only made her wolf salivate.

"How can you do that?" she asked as tears started to fill her eyes.

ARIEL DAWN

"Do what?" he said, his voice catching.

"Reject me? I know you feel this bond. I know you don't want to leave, that you want me. I can feel it in my bones, in your kiss. I can see it in your eyes, and yet, you fight it. Tell me how to fight this, and I will," she said as a single tear fell down her cheek.

"I'm not rejecting you, my darling Clementine," he said as he stepped closer to her, pulling her close.

She leaned her head on his sweaty chest, and she let the tears come. "It feels a lot like rejection, Malcolm," she said quietly.

"I'm saving you." His voice was soft as he held her.

"This isn't over," she said, knowing in her bones it was not. This was only the beginning. The vampires may have been taken out, but she knew they'd send more. They'd come back for her eventually.

Because their queen wanted her.

"I know," he said as he moved away. "The others will be back soon, we need to go. Get you and your Wolfman home."

"His name is Alaric," she said with a sniffle as she turned and slid into the passenger seat.

Mal rounded to the driver's side, taking his time as he got in the car. "What kind of a name is that?" Mal asked, making a face.

Cleo wiped her eyes. "It means all powerful ruler," she said.

"Of course it does," Mal said as he turned the car on, looking at Cleo once more. "Where to, darling?" he asked,

ARIEL DAWN

though the words felt heavy in the air.

A part of Cleo did not wish to answer. Wanted nothing more than to stall him, to protest. To hang on to this moment, this night, with Malcolm Crowley a little while longer.

But she also knew this would not be the last she'd see of her mate, and so she answered him.

***

When they'd arrived at Thorne Estate, she was surprised to see Sawyer standing out front.

"'Bout damn time you guys got back, I was starting to worry," he said as he chewed on a toothpick, looking almost as if he had no care in the world.

Malcolm opened the back door, gesturing to Sawyer. "He's a little out of it, but he should be okay. Vamps got a couple nibbles on him, but not enough to drain, I don't think. Still, he might need some rest," Mal ordered.

Cleo sat in the passenger seat, knowing each second was drawing closer and closer to the end. To the moment she didn't want to happen.

Sawyer leaned down and pulled Alaric up, the sounds of Alaric's pain and groans evident as they echoed in the air. "Starting to think you might be a cursed omega," Sawyer bit at her as she opened the door.

"I can assure you, I didn't cause this, I—" She started to speak, but Sawyer gave her the cold shoulder.

Mal set his hand on her shoulder, and the touch was calming, and she hated it, knowing it would be fleeting.

ARIEL DAWN

"It wasn't her fault. It—"

"Of course it was. They'll be back for her, the vamps. This is only the beginning, they won't stop until they get their precious omega's blood," Sawyer said as he helped Alaric through the door, turning to Cleo and Mal. "This war has only just begun," he said before turning and leading Alaric inside, leaving Cleo and Mal alone once more.

20

AS MALCOLM LOOKED at Cleo underneath the moonlight, wearing nothing but his tattered shirt, he felt at a crossroads. Vampires had come for everyone in his life and threatened to upend the balance once again.

A war between vampires and werewolves.

A war that would no doubt cause casualty among vamps, but also among wolves. Why such a thing mattered to him when he knew it shouldn't, only cemented the fact that he knew he needed to be as far from Cleo as possible, but yet...

"I guess this is the part where you walk away," Cleo said, her voice tinged with defeat.

"It is," Mal said as he leaned against the hood of his car.

"So why aren't you walking away?" she asked as she took a seat next to him.

"Because I don't know how," he said with an irritated laugh, running his hand over his face. "It's funny, you know. I've been with a lot of people, walked away from plenty of women in my short, thirty-one years, but when it comes to you, it's like my brain doesn't know how to process anything."

Cleo turned to him, looking up at him with vibrant eyes that made his heart flutter. "So stay," she pleaded.

"I can't. I need to find the vampires that killed my parents, I need to find a way to cure my sister's claim mark, and I need to—"

"I understand. You need to fight," she said with a sigh.

"Yeah, I do. I can't do that if I stay. And if I stay, I put you in danger."

"Danger will always be there, Malcolm. Whether you are here or not."

"Then maybe this won't be the last time we see each other," he said, feeling the stirring of hope within his chest.

Cleo turned to him, placing a soft kiss on his lips. "It won't be," she whispered against his lips, and then she left.

BLOOD OF MY ENEMY

Malcolm watched as she walked away slowly, into the darkness of the house, never looking back. He stood there for a moment, wondering if she'd turn around. If she'd run back into his arms, into his car, and perhaps they could ride off into the sunset together, but he knew it was wishful thinking.

And when he'd let the fantastical dream run its course, he hopped in the driver's side of his car, and took off for the Moonflower Motel, ready to let the darkness of slumber take all the pain and sadness away, even if it was only for a moment in time.

EPILOGUE

2 Months Later...

MALCOLM HATED THE snow just as much as he hated the heat, but most of all, he hated shoveling it.

Ava threw her backpack on as she trudged down the driveway toward the Impala, her keys in hand.

"I can't believe you're going out today," he grumbled as he hefted another load of snow into the pile on the side of the road.

"Adventure waits for no one, dear brother," she drawled sarcastically as she got into her car, starting it up.

"Seriously, who is crazy enough to venture out in this weather, the day before Christmas Eve?" he nipped.

"Don't be such a Grinch," she teased.

"Maybe by the time you come back, I'll have dug myself a trail to China and escaped all this fucking holiday nonsense," he said as he stopped for a moment to catch his breath.

"Well, if you're gone when I get back, I guess it'll be me and Mr. Jameson," she called out as she backed the car out onto the freshly plowed road.

"Be careful out there," he called back as he placed his hand on his hip.

ARIEL DAWN

"Uh-huh." She waved him off and headed out, going a little too fast for his liking.

He made his way back into the house, which felt too quiet. Mal walked the crisp, clean hallways, making his way to the kitchen, where he found Constance Chen, their aunt's housekeeper. Though the will stated that he and Ava would both inherit the house and Becky's estate, he couldn't grasp such an idea, but as he looked around, he let his mind wander.

Becky Lee Michaels never married, never had children. She'd lived her life as the rest of the Michaels had always done, doing the same thing. Her sister, Mal and Ava's mother, had been the black sheep, deciding to go against everything the Michaels had worked for, the life they'd built to escape the Crowley name. Yet, Lenora proudly wore the name and continued the family legacy of slaying the monsters in the shadows. Until one day they'd just... walked away. Changed their names like the rest of the family, walked away with their teenage son and an infant, and started a new life.

A normal life.

"How did they do it?" he asked out loud, forgetting he was not the only one in the room.

"I beg your pardon, Mal?" Connie spoke, jarring Malcolm from his thoughts.

He realized he was standing in the kitchen staring at the bare refrigerator, like a lunatic.

"Nothing, Connie, just thinking out

ARIEL DAWN

loud. Memories, you know."

Connie squinted at him, pursing her lips. She mumbled a string of Chinese that he did not understand.

Instead of trying, he continued to poke around in the refrigerator, looking for something to drink, not liking any of Ava's selections. In fact, there was barely anything other than three bottles of Bordeaux and an endless supply of bottled water. It was jarring to see the refrigerator so empty. Becky had always kept it stocked so well.

Her absence could be felt everywhere. Her death was sudden, too sudden. A heart attack, only a month after they'd arrived back from Mahoning. In her sleep, nonetheless.

It was still an adjustment for everyone, most of all Ava. Though she and Becky hadn't always gotten along or seen eye to eye on things, she was family, and it would be their first Christmas without her. She'd been the only living family they'd had left, that they knew of.

Now, it was just the two of them, a notion that made Malcolm very uneasy, made him feel rather torn.

He turned around, figuring the bar was probably better stocked than the refrigerator, thinking a drink might be better to soothe his soul.

And he was right.

He turned on the radio, fiddling with the buttons until he'd found a decent Classic Rock station, anything except the cheerful holiday music he loathed. He set about fixing a drink as the radio DJs rambled on and on about a show

ARIEL DAWN

coming to town.

Snow fell outside, and the warm lights around the outside of the house cast a golden glow that stirred up memories he'd been trying to forget for the past two months. He sighed, knowing it was no use to fight such things sober.

He pulled out the peach schnapps and a carton of half-empty orange juice from the mini fridge beneath the bar. Their aunt had always had a thing for screwdrivers, and the bar was always well stocked with orange juice, as the woman drank one every night after dinner.

When he finished making his fuzzy navel, he sat next to the window, watching the snow fall to the ground. One tiny snowflake melting into the sea of white, never to be seen again.

The ache in his heart did not cease. It hadn't since the moment he'd left Mahoning two months prior, and every time he'd pass someone on the street, in a crowded store, or bump into someone at a bar, his heart swelled with hope that maybe, just maybe...

Malcolm took a long pull of his drink, warring with himself not to go down that road.

His phone rang, and he knew the ringtone by heart.

"What's up, D?"

"Got a Christmas present for you," Dallas said with a snicker on the other end.

"A million dollars?" Mal teased.

"Better. I got us a gig performing over at the Vineyard Bar tomorrow night."

ARIEL DAWN

"On Christmas Eve?" Mal asked, surprised.

"What, like you have plans?" Dallas scoffed.

"Bold of you to assume I don't," Malcolm bit back as he took another sip of his drink.

"Got a date with the bottle and your right hand?" Dallas chuckled.

For the first time in forever, Mal didn't have a sarcastic remark.

Because the words hit him harder than any insult, any vampire bite.

He'd often relegated that this life was a lonely one, and he was all right with that. At least, he thought he was. Being alone meant no one could hurt you, and it also meant evil bloodsuckers couldn't hurt the ones you loved. The ones you'd do anything for.

BLOOD OF MY ENEMY

The ones who made your vision blurry, made your heart ache when they were a thousand miles away.

"Well, guess I'll have to reschedule. What time do we go on?" he said as he set down his glass with a shaky hand.

"Same time as always. Eight o'clock, sharp," Dallas said. "Oh, and that reminds me. You should bring Ava," Dallas said casually.

"I'm pretty sure she hates the band."

"Yeah, but it's Christmas Eve, man. She shouldn't be alone, not after— I mean, if she doesn't have anything going on."

Mal shrugged. Maybe Dallas was right, maybe the best thing for all of them, Ava included, was to keep moving, get away from this large, empty house. "Sure, I'll mention it."

ARIEL DAWN

"All right, I gotta go, man. Later." The click of the phone was instant, and Mal let out a breath.

"How did they do it?" he asked aloud again, staring at the glass, with just a fraction of drink left in it.

The familiar sounds of *Don't Fear the Reaper* filled the air, striking a chord within him.

"We can be like they are," he whispered to the air, a silent prayer, his mother's words filling him with a new determination.

"One day you'll understand," she mumbled as they sat on the porch, both taking drags of their cigarettes, smoke curling in the wind.

Mal continued to watch the sun, staring as a few stray silhouettes of bikes rode off into the distance.

BLOOD OF MY ENEMY

The sun lit up the snow, shades of gold and orange as the song droned on about being able to fly, imploring him to not be afraid.

And in that moment, Malcolm Crowley found his courage in the depths of his heart, in the steady ache that told him he was alive.

So he picked up the phone and dialed Hunter.

"Hey, Mal, what's up?" he asked, the sounds of a crowd behind him making his voice slightly difficult to hear.

"Can you find someone for me? Like, an address or a phone number..."

"Absolutely, I just need a name, and any other information you might have."

"Clementine Srirocco." He licked his lips, watching as the sun disappeared behind the trees once more. "Location,

ARIEL DAWN

I'm not sure, but possibly... Mahoning."

A pause on the phone until Hunter spoke made Mal nervous. "Clementine Srirocco. All right, got it. I'm out with Tito at the moment, grabbing some last minute stuff, but I'll get back to you probably tonight, if that's okay."

Mal nodded as his chest swelled with hope. "Yup, perfect. Thanks, Hunter."

"Don't mention it, Mal. Oh, by the way, I uh... I did some digging like you asked... about that coven, the Boracellis?"

"Find anything interesting?" he asked as he watched a cardinal land on the windowsill.

"Actually, yeah. I did," Hunter replied.

"Well, shoot."

"I thought it was interesting to note that the Boracellis have acquired quite a bit of territory since the '20s in my initial findings."

"Why is that interesting?" Mal asked, unsure of where he was going with such information.

What did territory have to do with anything?

"Because, apparently, if my sources are correct... parts of Chester U sit on the edge of Boracelli territory, and so does Mahoning."

"You're right, that is quite interesting. Thank you, Hunter."

"No problem, Mal. I'll call you later when I get that number and address for you."

Mal ended the call, turning over the information in his brain, trying to figure it all out, feeling like the answers were just out of reach.

ARIEL DAWN

He drained the last of his drink, slamming the glass down when he was done. The sun shone brightly against the windowpane, the snow glittering in its presence like twinkling stars in the sky, and Malcolm was certain of one thing.

Cleo was right.

This was only the beginning.

He felt on the edge of a precipice, with more questions than answers, but nevertheless, he felt determined. For if there was one thing Malcolm Crowley knew how to do, it was fight, and so he vowed to himself that he would do whatever it took to find the courage to do what his parents did. He would do what they had died trying to do.

Protect his family and his friends and build a life they'd be proud of.

***

BLOOD OF MY ENEMY

Malcolm blew a ring of smoke in the chilly winter air on the front porch, gazing up at the clear, winter night sky. The stars were bright, reminding him of all the years he'd spent camping as a youth, gazing up at the star-filled sky in the middle of the woods, and how his father would point out constellations, telling him all the stories about the stars.

His favorite had always been that of Lupus, the wolf, which was only visible to him on those mountain camping trips.

Looking now at the cluster of stars, remembering such things only made him want to see it again, but it was out of reach.

A vibration shook in his pocket, jostling him from his strange star-filled trance, and he swiped to see his notification. It was Hunter.

Mal opened the text immediately, his heart stopping. He stared at the string of numbers below Clementine Srirocco's name, frozen in time and space.

He didn't think.

He only acted, impulse taking over.

Desire built within him, leading to wishful thinking. All the stars in the sky filled him with the courage he had somehow forgotten about.

Three rings sounded, and Malcolm started to think that perhaps, it was a stupid idea.

After all, it was the holidays. It wasn't like he expected her to be waiting by the phone or anything. It was a whim, nothing more. It was—

"Hello?" A soft, sweet voice filled his

ears, and instantly it was as if a weight had been lifted off his shoulders. His muscles eased, his pulse returning to normal from its anxiety-ridden state, and his insides felt strangely warm at just the sound of her voice.

His mate.

"Hey," was all he could muster at the moment as the feelings overtook him.

Some bonds were stronger than blood, after all, and Malcolm intended to get down to the bottom of it all, one way or another, come hell or high water.

Thank you for reading!

The Goon Squad will return in Blood Of The Lost, The Hunter Games #2

The Thorne Brothers & Cleo will return in Thorne Of Blood, The Hunter Games #3, coming soon!

Turn the page now for a taste of Blood Of The Lost...

PREVIEW

THE AIR WAS thick with broken promises, tainted memories, and the scent of blood. The sound of Ava's screams would haunt Dallas for the rest of his undead life.

Because as Dallas lay motionless on the blood-soaked ground of the Marquis, suspended in motion between life and death, he could feel his insides hardening, changing.

BLOOD OF MY ENEMY

Like a moth inside a cocoon, all he could do was wait. For the transition to take hold.

"Get up," the sound of a woman's voice called to him, but he did not recognize it.

Dallas tried to move his fingers, his toes, but everything felt heavy.

He grunted in response as his eyelashes fluttered. The room he was in was dark, the only light the bright flash from a phone screen.

"Fucking shut that off," he growled, stretching his fingers. He moved his hand to shield his eyes. The light was so bright, blinding almost.

"Oh, this one's got spunk," another woman's voice carried excitedly.

"Who do you think is responsible for making him?"

ARIEL DAWN

Dallas attempted to move his legs, the effort nearly exhausting.

His entire body felt as if he'd been hit by a freight train. He held his hand in front of his eyes, noting the mess of blood all over his skin.

Memories filtered back into his brain.

The Djinn heading for Ava and Mal.

How he'd pushed them out of the way, without a second thought.

There had been so much blood…

Dallas ran his hands over his chest, feeling for the gaping wound he knew should be there.

But he felt no such thing, just cold, congealed blood, and soft, sore skin among the shredded remains of his costume.

"Can you get up?"

Dallas's gaze settled on one of the

women, the one with the excited voice.

She kneeled before him, long raven waves falling over her shoulders. Her pale skin and glowing aquamarine eyes were indicative of her breed of monster.

Djinn.

She looked strangely familiar...

Dallas leaned in close to the Djinn, letting her scent fill his airways. She smelled of woods and citrus and he could feel her natural siren aura trying to capture him.

"You got a name, sweetheart, or should I just call you mine?" he asked, the words empty, soulless. It wasn't anything he hadn't done before, but this time... it felt different.

Because there was only one woman he wanted to call his, and he'd left her with the vampire who'd claimed her

ARIEL DAWN

blood...

The Djinn giggled.

Fucking giggled like an innocent child.

"You can call me—"

"Midnight?" Her name came to him without warning as the memories flooded him.

"Oh! You're the guy from the bar... the...hunter..." she said as her eyes widened in surprise.

"He's a hunter?" the other woman shrieked, and Dallas's gaze was pulled away. The other Djinn resembled Midnight, though she was taller with short chin length black hair that boasted bright blue streaks.

"Ami will have a field day with him..."

Midnight pursed her lips as she set her hand on his shoulder, imploring him with her gaze.

BLOOD OF MY ENEMY

"Perhaps he could be of use to us... to Ami," Midnight said as she tugged Dallas's sleeve.

"Can you get up?" she asked again, her voice soft.

Dallas wiggled his toes in his boots, bending his legs and knees slowly. They still ached, but feeling had come back. He motioned forward, getting up too fast as he started to feel dizzy.

"I'm fine..." he bit, shaking off the touch of the sweet-voiced Djinn.

He could hear the sounds of sirens in the distance, and he knew they were right. He did need to move.

He needed to find Malcolm, Ava...

The thought of the Crowleys caused an ache in his heart as his stomach twisted in nauseous knots.

He was starving. He grabbed his

stomach, a painful growl escaping his throat.

"What the fuck..."

"He needs to eat," Midnight protested.

"The damn police will be here any minute, Midnight!" the other one bit out.

Dallas jumped as Midnight slid her hand in his, tugging him toward her.

"Whoever made him doesn't look like they're coming back. He's one of us now. I won't leave him to the fucking wolves."

Dallas tried to make sense of her words, but he couldn't. His head was pounding, his body aching, and he was *starving*. His gaze fell on the short vixen in front of him, his mouth going dry.

I wish...

The sound of doors opening, of rushed footsteps, told them all they needed to know.

BLOOD OF MY ENEMY

And so, Jake Dallas followed the Djinn into the shadows, escaping into the night.

Find Blood Of The Lost at your favorite online retailer.

If you enjoyed this book, you may also enjoy the Shifters of Starfall Creek.

Start the series now with Hollow's Sunrise.

Hollow's Sunrise

Jade Hollow wants more. More than a life as an Alpha's female. More than spending forever in Starfall Creek. She wants to rule the pack. Reverie Jacob's life is as normal as it gets... until he witnesses something he shouldn't and finds himself in the middle of his wildest dreams. His friend is a wolf... The hottest girl he's ever seen seems to be into him... Two very unimaginable, but real things.

Dustin Blackridge has been waiting his whole life to be the Alpha of the Hollow Pack—after all, he's been in love with Jade since they were kids. Nothing and no one will stop him from getting what he wants. When a pain in the ass human shows up on Hollow's ground

BLOOD OF MY ENEMY

and threatens to ruin everything, Dustin needs to handle it. And quickly. Dustin must decide where his loyalties lie... with Jade or with his pack. Will unexpected love get in the way of what they want?

Hollow's Sunrise is book ONE in the Shifters of Starfall Creek series and ends on a cliffhanger. This series is best read in order. It is a shifter, why choose romance with mature themes, situations, and language.

Hollow's Sunset

Her love will join the divided.
Their love will be legendary.

Jade Hollow's transgressions are stacking up...

When the elders show up on Hollow's ground, Jade's world will never be the same.

She must answer for her crimes—turning Reverie, starting her own pack, and challenging alpha Dustin for the right to rule as Hollow's alpha.

But Jade isn't the only one with trials to overcome.

Dustin, Reverie, and Ranger find themselves facing a whole new set of

BLOOD OF MY ENEMY

obstacles together as the countdown to the trials commences.

Will their legendary love be enough to overcome it all?

Hollow's Legacy

This is our fight. This is our legacy.

In the wake of passing the Strength Trial, Jade Hollow finds herself in uncharted waters.

Loyalties and pack bonds are being tested under the watchful eye of the elders as Jade prepares for the Mind Trials, judged by none other than Samuel Blackridge—who isn't quite ready to let go of his lifelong ambition to replace the Hollow Pack as the leading pack in Starfall.

As the prophecy comes full circle, and the rise of the Legacy Pack brings forth a new dawn in Starfall Creek, Dustin, Reverie, and Ranger soon find they have more to defend than just their legendary

BLOOD OF MY ENEMY

love... and they aren't going to go down without a fight.

Hollow's Legacy is book THREE in the Shifters of Starfall Creek series and ends with a HEA.
This series is best read in order.
It is a shifter, why choose romance with mature themes, situations, and language.

OTHER BOOKS BY ARIEL DAWN

The Hunter Games

Blood Of My Enemy

Blood Of The Lost

Thorne Of Blood

Speed Dating with the Denizens of the Underworld Series

Hecate

Hades

Orion

Athena

Spike

The Forevermore Series

In The Cards

In The Blood

In The Shadows

BLOOD OF MY ENEMY

In The Deep
In The Garden
In The Night-coming soon!

Shifters Of Starfall Creek Series

Hollow's Sunrise

Hollow's Sunset

Hollow's Legacy

Shifters of Starfall Creek Collection: Books 1-3

Sign up for Ariel Dawn's newsletter and claim your sweet treat!
https://mailchi.mp/e5f326e433bf/dawn-breaks-official-newsletter

CONNECT WITH ARIEL DAWN

Website

http://www.ariel-dawn.com/

Goodreads:

http://www.goodreads.com/authorarieldawn

Bookbub:

http://www.bookbub.com/authors/ariel-dawn

Facebook:

http://www.facebook.com/authorarieldawn

Twitter:

https://twitter.com/ArielDawn10

Join Dusk Chasers—Ariel Dawn's Official Readers Group for access to exclusive content!

ABOUT ARIEL DAWN

USA TODAY BESTSELLING AUTHOR Ariel Dawn grew up as an avid reader and is a creative soul.

What started out as writing reviews for indie romance authors led to featuring quirky, stereotypical, and weird covers on her Instagram Wrong Turn Romance, which gave her the courage to finally decide to live her dream and become an author.

Ariel writes plot driven paranormal romance and hopes to venture into fantasy and rom-com in the future. When she isn't writing, she can be found cosplaying, attending conventions, creating all sorts of artwork in her studio, or editing photos for her photography business.

A self-professed geek and foodie, she loves hanging out with family and friends and playing video games and board games with her retro gamer husband.

Made in the USA
Middletown, DE
24 August 2024